Jack Venables

Samantha Wheeler lives in Brisbane with her family and many animals. Her first story took shape during a writing course at the Queensland Writers Centre in 2009 and was accepted into the inaugural Allen & Unwin Children's Manuscript Development Program in 2010. She went on to have a short story published in the *One Book Many Brisbanes* anthology and to write *Smooch & Rose*, her first children's book, inspired by a local strawberry farm and her concern for Queensland's koalas.

www.samanthawheeler.com

Samantha Wheeler

First published 2013 by University of Queensland Press
PO Box 6042, St Lucia, Queensland 4067 Australia
Reprinted 2014

www.uqp.com.au
uqp@uqp.uq.edu.au

Cover design and illustrations by Aileen Lord
Typeset in 13/20 pt Adobe Garamond by Post Pre-press Group, Brisbane
Printed in Australia by McPherson's Printing Group

Cataloguing-in-Publication Data
National Library of Australia

Wheeler, Samantha, author.
Smooch & Rose / Samantha Wheeler.

ISBN 978 0 7022 4986 0 (pbk)
ISBN 978 0 7022 5168 9 (pdf)
ISBN 978 0 7022 5169 6 (epub)
ISBN 978 0 7022 5170 2 (kindle)

For children.

Nature conservation – Juvenile fiction.

A823.4

*For my mum and all the extra-ordinary grans
in my life.*

1. Rescue

We found Smooch last strawberry season. I'd just started on my maths homework when I heard fierce barks outside. Lizzie, our Jack Russell, raced to the back door with her ears pricked and her tail between her legs. It was already pitch-black, but Gran and I peered out the door, as if by magic we'd be able to see through the dark.

'Grab the torches, Rosie,' said Gran. 'We'd better take a look.' Without even blinking, she pulled on her gumboots and tugged on her coat. My gran wasn't like ordinary grandmothers. She lived in strawberry-stained overalls and wore thick gumboots coated in the red clay soil from our farm.

Together we crossed the damp, dewy paddocks. The barking grew louder. When we were close to the creek, Lizzie began to growl. Soon all the hackles on her back stood up. Frenzied barking echoed all around us. It sounded like two dogs or three or maybe even four. And they sounded like they were onto something.

Really onto something.

'Ratbags,' whispered Gran. She bent down and scooped Lizzie up, just in case. Lizzie was small and getting old. She wouldn't stand a chance against a pack of blood-hungry dogs.

I huddled next to Gran and peered grimly into the dark. The winter's air was even colder down among the trees and I wished, like her, I'd thrown on my coat. I hugged my arms around me.

A terrifying, high-pitched squeal shattered the air. My skin prickled. My heart thumped against my rib cage.

'What was that?' I croaked.

'A possum, I'd say,' said Gran, shining her torch into the bushes. She stepped forwards and squinted into the circle of yellow torchlight.

I hung back. My legs had turned to jelly. How many dogs were there? What if they turned on us?

Then Gran did something unexpected. 'GET OUT OF HERE!' she shouted, in a deep growly voice.

I jumped.

'GO ON, GET OUT! GET HOME!'

The barking stopped. Just like that. Branches swayed and twigs snapped as the dogs scampered off through the bushes. Finally, it was quiet again.

Imagine that! Wild, crazy dogs – afraid of my gran!

When we were sure they had gone, Gran rushed into the bushes, her torch swinging from side to side. Then she stopped and handed me Lizzie. Lizzie's belly was soaked from the damp grass and her heart raced against mine.

Gran stooped and shone the torch on the long grass. Fresh red blood stained the blades.

And then I saw it.

A large koala was huddled against the base of a tree. Black terrified eyes shone like wet pebbles in Gran's light. Grey furry sides heaved in and out. Its mouth hung open, panting in fear. The dogs must have shaken it around. My throat grew tight, making it hard to swallow. The koala stared at me, blinking slowly. Begging me to help.

Gran took off her coat and wrapped up the koala. 'It's okay,' she murmured. 'We've got you now. We'll keep you safe.'

I hugged Lizzie close. I hoped Gran was right.

The vet surgery was closed for the night. Gran rang the after hours bell and our vet, Craig, opened the door. He looked troubled when he saw the large bundle in Gran's arms. 'Sit down a moment, Mrs Nunn,' he said, taking the koala. 'I'll have a quick look.'

Gran and I sat on one of the cold wooden benches in the waiting room. The fluoro lights hurt my eyes. They seemed too bright after all the black outside. Gran breathed too loudly. The clock on the wall ticked too slowly:

7.15

7.16

7.17.

'Do you think it'll be alright, Gran?' I whispered.

Gran sucked in her lips. 'Don't get your hopes up, love,' she said. 'It'll take a miracle to save that one, I think.'

I forced myself to read the posters on the wall. There were pictures of ticks and worms and stuff about choosing the right food for your dog. But my brain wouldn't work. I could think of only the koala and nothing else. I jumped when the surgery door swung open.

Craig's arms were empty.

'Sorry, Mrs Nunn. Sorry, Rose,' he said, shaking his head. 'She didn't make it.'

Gran wrapped her arms around me and gave me a squeeze.

'There's one more thing,' Craig added. 'Did you see her baby?'

I pulled away from Gran. A baby?

'There was milk in the koala's pouch. I think she might have had a baby riding on her back when the dogs attacked her. You didn't see anything?'

'No, there was no baby. I mean . . . it was dark . . . there were so many dogs,' I stammered. 'We didn't . . .'

Gran squeezed my arm. 'Shhh Rosie, it's okay.'

'A baby won't stand a chance out there on its own,' said Craig. 'If you do find it, wrap it up warmly and bring it straight back in.'

I nodded. A tiny baby koala. Out there, all alone, in the dark? We had to go find it. 'Come on, Gran,' I said, tugging at the waiting room door. 'What if we're too late?'

2. Smooch

Gran and I locked Lizzie up in the house before grabbing an old towel and running back to the creek. The frogs and crickets were making such a racket that we had to listen hard for sounds from a frightened baby koala. Gran shone the torch around the trees as we squinted in the dark. Spindly spider webs glistened in the torchlight. Fat warty toads scuttled by our feet. Where was the little joey?

I was about to give up when I saw something move near the base of a skinny gum tree.

'There it is!' I cried. A bundle of white and grey fur was trying to clamber up the tree. We watched in horror as the koala kept slipping down the trunk. Maybe its claws were too weak. Maybe it was injured. It let out a terrified squeal as we approached, but Gran threw the towel over its head and it seemed to calm down.

'We won't hurt you,' Gran whispered, wrapping up the baby. At the car, she passed the precious parcel to me. Its trembling body was light and I could feel its heart thudding through the towel. I held it on my lap like a pile of fragile eggs, my fingers cupped around it and my thumbs rested on top.

'It's so little,' I said, making sure I didn't grip it too tight. 'So special.'

'Just goes to show, Rosie love, it's true what I always say: things don't have to be big to be special.'

I looked down in wonder and tipped my thumbs back enough for the towel to open a slither. One small round ear poked out. I ran my thumb very carefully over the soft white fur.

'Will it die?' I asked.

Gran shook her head. 'Hope not. Let's see what Craig says.'

'But it hasn't got a mum now. I mean, how will it survive and how . . .'

I had about 5,000 questions, but Gran told me to concentrate on one thing at a time and focus on holding the koala. 'We're all it's got now, Rosie, so make sure you keep it safe.'

Craig was waiting for us when we arrived. He eased the baby from my arms and disappeared out the back. A few minutes later he came out to tell us the news.

'He's a healthy joey, about eight months old,' he said. 'He isn't injured, but he's too young to return to the wild without his mother.'

I stepped in closer. 'Can I keep him?' I said. 'I would look after him, I promise. I already look after a horse and a goat and some chooks . . .'

'Rosie,' said Gran, frowning.

'Please?'

Craig shook his head. 'You need a special permit to care for wildlife. We'll need to find him a licensed carer. But don't worry, if all goes well, they'll release him again, usually in the same place he was found. It could be a while until he's big enough, perhaps even a year. Afterwards you'll be able to see him every day.'

A year? I didn't want to wait a whole *year*. That was forever away. I wanted to care for the koala *now*. I folded my arms and scowled. I wished we'd never brought the baby to the vet's.

'Come on, love,' said Gran, propelling me towards the door. 'I'm sure Craig will give the carer our details. Perhaps they'll let you visit the joey.'

We drove home in silence. I glared out the window. I could have looked after the baby koala. I'd been helping Gran out on the farm ever since Mum and Dad had died. It had been nearly four years since their accident and now I knew everything there was to know about animals. I looked after Sally, our goat, even if she chased me and headbutted me half the time. It was my job to feed and rug Mickey, Dad's old racehorse, who'd grown so old I had to chop his carrots up extra small in his mash; and it was me who locked up the chooks and collected their eggs. Then there was Lizzie, of course. Surely I could care for one little koala? I leant my forehead against the cold glass of the window. Somehow I'd have to show them I could do it.

I headed straight for the vet surgery on my way to school the next morning. The waiting room looked different in the daylight.

'Has the carer come yet?' I asked the lady at reception. I had to convince her to give the koala to me.

'The carer?' the receptionist asked, frowning at me over the top of the counter.

'For the baby koala. We brought him in last night.'

'Yes, he was picked up about an hour ago. Is there a problem?'

My mouth dropped open. I was too late. The koala was gone.

'Oh,' I mumbled. 'No problem.' But there *was* a problem. A huge problem. *I* should be the one caring for the joey. Not some stranger. He'd remember me and I'd make him feel safe.

I stomped the rest of the way to school. What if the carer didn't feed the koala properly? What if he missed his mum and the carer didn't cuddle him enough?

I dragged my feet through the school gates. School was the last place I wanted to be. It was becoming just like the rest of Redland Bay. People and buildings everywhere. Developers were gobbling up all the spare bushland and turning the old farms into ugly housing estates. City people were flocking to the area for 'green changes' and 'tree changes' and their kids were filling up our school. There were temporary classrooms shoved in every which way and new teachers constantly asking to be shown around. They didn't know anything about anyone and they didn't understand a thing about Redland Bay.

But worse than the crowding, the new kids were different. They had mobiles and laptops and iPads and 3D TVs. All the stuff I'd never had. All the stuff I didn't want. The girls squabbled over lipgloss and obsessed about shopping and boy bands, while the boys spent more time on their hair than I did. I found it best to keep out of everyone's way.

'Hey, Nunn, been sleeping in a stable lately?' Kellee and Tahlia stood at the bag racks. They'd been huddled over Tahlia's phone, but looked up when they heard me arrive.

'Yeah, Nunn. Grass for lunch again?'

I pushed my bag into a spare spot on the rack, hoping the bell would hurry up.

'What's up, goat got your tongue?' sniggered Kellee. She and Tahlia had moved into the new townhouses at the back of Gran's farm last year, where Mr Douglas's fruit farm used to be. At first, I'd asked if they wanted to come over and meet our animals, but they'd laughed and said animals were for bumpkins. Besides, they said, they were way too busy with Maths Club and training for the netball team to hang out with scarecrows like me.

I didn't ask them over again.

Tahlia whispered to Kellee, who pursed her lips and took a step towards me. Her shoulders were level with my chin. They would be. She was goal shooter for the school team. I backed up against the bag racks. I wished I were invisible. Or could disappear like a joey into its mum's pouch.

'Good morning, everyone. Come on inside. Rose, glad to see you made it to school on time today.' Our teacher was new and she hardly glanced at us as we trooped inside. Kellee and Tahlia barged ahead of me. 'Get you later,' they sneered before making their way to their desks at the back.

After the roll, we had to copy down notes about 'habitat' and 'food chains' from the interactive whiteboard. Copying was always tricky for me. I sat up the front so I could see the board properly, but it took me so long to make sure I hadn't made any spelling mistakes, I hardly ever got all the notes written down. I soon gave up and looked out the window instead.

A big old gum tree stood outside our classroom and a light breeze fluttered through its leaves. They rustled softly, just like they did down by our creek. What had happened to the baby koala? Who had taken him and were they treating him right?

I didn't have to wait long to find out. After school that afternoon, there was a loud knock on our door. When I opened it, a short slim lady with bleached blonde hair stood on our steps.

'Hi, I'm Carol,' she said, bending to pat Lizzie. When she straightened, she held out her hand to shake mine. She was the only person I'd ever met whose hands looked more worn than Gran's. They were just as brown as Gran's too. 'The vet gave me your address. I'm the wildlife carer who adopted the baby koala. I was hoping to collect some gum-leaves from the trees down at your creek.'

I glared at her. So *she* was the one who'd taken *my* koala. 'We found him,' I muttered angrily. 'We should be caring for him. We know what he needs.'

'I know you found him,' she said. Her face was nearly as leathery as her hands, but her eyes crinkled kindly when she smiled. 'Craig told me. Well done, you. And what a lovely healthy boy he is too. I've named him Smooch, by the way, since he loves a cuddle so much.'

My frowning face relaxed a little. I hadn't even thought about naming him. And Smooch was perfect. A baby koala named after a cuddle.

Carol smiled. 'It's hard work caring for these little guys. It'll take a bit to get him on track. I could do with a hand, to be honest.'

My frowny face completely melted away. Carol did seem nice. 'Can *I* help?'

'Sure thing. How's Saturday?'

I grinned. Saturday couldn't come fast enough.

3. Carol's Place

It had been my idea to open a stall to sell damaged strawberries. We sold 'Nunn's Famous Strawberries' for three dollars a kilo out the front of our place every Saturday during strawberry season. We had no shortage of customers since our tiny farm had become squashed in between all the new houses in Wellington Point. We weren't too far from anything anymore. People could easily wander over and pick out a punnet or two. It turned out that city people liked farm-fresh strawberries, even if they were funny shapes and sizes. Probably because they still tasted of sunshine. It was kind of nice seeing all those reject berries making people happy instead of ending up on the compost heap. And, of course, Gran was pleased to see the extra cash.

The Saturday after Carol dropped by, I couldn't wait to close up the stall. The minute the last punnet sold, I raced down to the creek and collected an armful of leaves. I practically ran the whole three blocks to Carol's house.

'I brought these,' I said, trying not to puff. 'I hope they're okay.' I'd also brought my teddy, Brownie, just in case Smooch was pining for his mum. It had been a present when Mum and Dad died and always did the trick when I was missing them.

Carol reached for the leaves and beckoned me inside. 'Good on you. Just what we need.'

I peered around the front room. I couldn't see any baby koalas – just Carol's unusually large belly.

Carol caught me looking. 'You didn't think I'd been scoffing ice-creams, did you?' she said,

18

reaching into the bottom of her jumper. She used both hands to ease out a round bundle wrapped up in a T-shirt. Two grey and white fluffy ears appeared from the bundle. Two bright button eyes followed.

'I told your little man you were coming,' she said. 'Here, sit down on the couch. Have a look at the beautiful bub you found.'

Smooch *was* beautiful. His furry face looked up trustingly at me as Carol placed him gently on my lap. White hairs stuck out of his ears, like an old man who'd just got out of bed. His black-brown eyes were ringed with white and his fur was springy, like the wool on a woolly sheep. He was a real, live teddy bear. So perfect, so soft.

I didn't know where to put my hands. They seemed big and clunky next to Smooch. He was about the size of the Beanie Babies the other girls brought to school and must have weighed about the same as a kilo punnet of strawberries. But he was way better than strawberries. I didn't want to hurt him so I sat statue still.

'You're doing good,' said Carol, nodding at me. 'Real good. But maybe breathe now, hey?'

I took a breath and as I did Smooch looked up at my shoulder. He stared for a second and then lifted his front paws, like he was going to grab at my neck. I stiffened. Was he going to bite me?

'It's okay,' said Carol when she saw my frozen face. 'He wants to snuggle, that's all. Relax. Just see what he does.' Smooch reached his claws up and gripped onto my jumper. I held my breath again. He crawled up my chest and then onto my shoulder. My hair hung loose in a tangled mess and Smooch reached for it, his soft fur brushing against my chin. He wriggled around the back of my neck until he was comfortably nestled in my hair. He wasn't heavy and his claws weren't sharp, but I wasn't sure what to do. What do you do when there's a koala in your hair?

'It's okay, he won't hurt you,' said Carol. She offered Smooch a fresh gumleaf. 'Come on, buddy, it's not nap time. Don't you want your lunch?' He reluctantly untangled himself and took the leaf between one finger and his first tiny thumb. He sat on my lap, nibbling the leaf daintily, as if he wasn't really sure what it was.

'In the wild, koala babies learn to eat solid food when they're about six months old,' Carol told me. 'They start with something called pap. It's basically their mum's poo.'

I screwed up my nose. 'Eugh. Really? Poo?'

Carol laughed at my funny face. 'Oh, it's not that bad. It's how the mums pass on good bacteria for their bub's stomach. Smooch's mum already started him on it before she died, so his stomach can handle gumleaves. If she hadn't, they'd be poisonous for him. Pretty smart, hey?'

It took Smooch ages to eat just three leaves. His mouth was small and he chewed very slowly. When he lost interest, he ditched the leaf he was holding and clambered unsteadily off the couch. Once he was down, he waddled over to where Brownie lay on the floor. He sniffed him and then pounced, wrestling the teddy and trying to bite his ears. Brownie fell sideways on top of Smooch and I sprang from my seat.

'He'll be okay,' said Carol, beckoning for me to sit back down. 'He's just playing. I think your teddy does remind him of his mum.'

I smiled. I understood completely. Although I'd never exactly wrestled Brownie, I knew how nice it was to have a big brown bear to cuddle. I was glad I'd chosen to give Brownie to Smooch now.

After he'd played for a while, Smooch was ready for another sleep. Carol said koalas slept a lot. She carefully bundled him up in her make-do pouch and popped him back inside her jumper.

'Will you come back next Saturday?' she asked as I stood up to go. 'Meet the rest of my babies?'

There were more? My eyes grew wide. I quickly nodded. 'Yes, please,' I said. 'I'll bring more leaves.'

After I'd said goodbye, I ran the whole way home. I couldn't wait to tell Gran and Lizzie all about Carol and Smooch. I wondered what it would take to become a wildlife carer. Perhaps Carol could train me and then I could do it too? My head began to explode with possibilities. Imagine all the animals we could fit on the farm. Imagine caring for animals like Smooch – for the rest of my life!

4. Bush Babies

Strawberry season came around only once a year. It was the best time of year because we got to fill our bellies with fresh juicy strawberries, but it was also the worst time because it was winter and always cold. Our big old verandah wrapped all the way around our creaky timber house and with the huge ancient trees crowding up over our roof, practically no sun got in. It was a dark house at that time of year and the first thing Gran and I did every afternoon was switch on the bright cheery lights in the kitchen.

'Hey, guess what?' I shouted when I got home from Carol's late that afternoon. Strange. Gran hadn't turned on any lights. Even though it was nearly time for tea. I threw my runners off in the hall and flicked the switch in the kitchen.

My hand froze at the wall. Gran sat at the kitchen table, her head buried in her hands.

'Gran?'

She looked up at me and blinked against the yellow light. Her eyes were red, like she'd been crying.

I started towards her. But then I stopped. A torn envelope sat beside her elbow on the table. A piece of scrunched-up paper lay on the floor by her feet.

'What's happened?' I asked, not daring to take another step. The envelope wasn't bright and colourful, like a birthday card or party invitation. It was slim and white and crisp. And very serious-looking.

It must have been. Gran never cried.

Gran rummaged in her pocket for a tissue and quickly blew her nose. 'It's okay, Rosie,' she said. 'Just that . . . things are a bit tough, that's all.

The bills are mounting up, the strawberry price is down, and now this.' Her eyes fell to the envelope. It might have been a huge black hairy huntsman the way she looked at it. 'It's from the bank. I've been expecting it for months. Your Uncle Malcolm said this would happen.'

I gritted my teeth. Uncle Malcolm! He was Dad's younger brother and he lived in the city. It had been hard for Gran to care for me and run the farm after Mum and Dad died, so Gran had asked Uncle Malcolm for help. He was always too busy selling big city houses to rich city people, so he'd given Gran money instead.

But last year people stopped buying big houses in the city and Uncle Malcolm ran out of money to spare. He started ringing up Gran every week, telling her to sell the farm and cut her losses. He wanted Gran and me to move in with him so he could keep an eye on us.

But Gran told him no.

She said she'd *never* sell the farm.

Uncle Malcolm wouldn't let Lizzie come if we

moved in with him. He was allergic to everything. *Everything!* And that included dogs, even smart ones with soft brown eyes and a taste for berries.

Uncle Malcolm had become furious when Gran said no. He shouted at her, a loud booming shout that made our timber windows rattle. A shout that still gave me nightmares. 'You're being ridiculous!' he'd roared. 'The bank will come knocking. Dog or no dog. Give it time, you'll see!'

I'd hugged Brownie close the night Uncle Malcolm had shouted at Gran. We'd never leave Lizzie behind. Would we?

And now it seemed Uncle Malcolm had been right. The bank *had* come knocking. I looked at Gran's face, all crumpled and red. They couldn't make us move. I wouldn't let them.

'Don't worry, Gran,' I assured her, using my bravest voice. 'We don't need Uncle Malcolm. Something'll come up. It'll be okay.' I tried to sound upbeat, but Gran didn't look convinced. I crossed my fingers behind my back.

*

The following Saturday took forever to arrive. When it finally did, and the strawberry stall had sold out, I gathered an armful of leaves and headed to Carol's. This time Lizzie came too. At first Carol wasn't sure about having a dog inside, but it wasn't long before she realised that Lizzie wasn't an ordinary old dog and let her stay.

We met Jedda, the kangaroo joey who slept in a knitted red jumper with the bottom sewn up, and Pip, the wallaby so young she looked like a tiny pink bird. Then there was Maggie, the magpie who could dribble a soccer ball with her beak, and Ned and Nellie and Piggy and . . . There were so many animals, I lost count! They all loved Lizzie, especially Smooch, who thought I'd brought him another teddy bear to wrestle. Carol told me she'd been caring for injured or orphaned animals for over 30 years.

That explained her worn-out hands.

Bunny rugs and blankets were tossed over every surface in Carol's house. The kitchen bench was completely hidden under bottles of formula and bags of green pellets and boxes of birdseed. The whole place smelt of warm soggy Weet-Bix.

'What do you have to do to become a wildlife carer?' I asked. 'Do you have to go to university?' I bit my lip and reached down to rub between Lizzie's ears. I wasn't smart like Kellee and Tahlia. I'd never got an 'A' in my life. 'It's just that . . . well . . . I'm not that good at school. Do you think, maybe I . . .'

'You rescued Smooch, didn't you? You'd breeze it in,' said Carol. 'These guys need caring people exactly like you.' She scratched her head with her wide brown hands. 'As long as you don't mind smelling of baby formula, that is, and getting no sleep, never having a holiday and . . . oh . . . having no money. What do you think?'

I laughed and scooped Lizzie into my arms. I didn't mind how I smelt. And having no money or holidays? That was old news at our place. I nodded happily. 'Yes, yes, I'd love to.' Lizzie licked my face in approval.

Carol shrugged. 'Tell you what, why not practise

right now? Smooch is ready for a snooze. You can be mum. Go on, tuck your T-shirt in.'

I released Lizzie in a flurry and jammed my T-shirt into my jeans. Carol snuggled Smooch up in his pouch and passed me the bundle. With trembling hands, I slid it down the neck of my T-shirt until it was safely nestled against my skin, just above the waistband of my jeans. Now I had a Santa belly just like Carol. My cheeks ached from my massive grin.

I stood perfectly still, feeling Smooch's gentle breathing tickle my tummy. I couldn't budge. What if I woke him? What if he got hurt? Carol eventually convinced me that it was okay to move, saying there was too much to do to just stand around like a lump. She passed me some ointment to rub on Pip the wallaby, asked me to cut up apples for the possums, and then showed me how to make up a bowl of warm cereal. 'For Jedda,' she said. 'We're trying to fatten her up.'

Jedda's red jumper was slung across the back of a chair. The neck hung open like the opening to a pouch. I wasn't sure what I was supposed to do. Pull her out? What if I frightened her?

'Jedda,' I said gently, crouching awkwardly beside the jumper. 'Lunchtime.' The jumper moved. A small pointed brown face appeared through the neck hole. Two enormous ears poked out. Jedda's wet nose twitched in the direction of my bowl. Not long afterwards, her whole body emerged from the jumper. Her back legs were long and spindly with the knobbliest knees I'd ever seen. She had three toes on each foot. Then came her never-ending tail. Her shiny eyes stared at the cereal.

I smiled. Lizzie lay on the floor beside me while I scooped a small amount of cereal onto the spoon and offered it to the hungry kangaroo. The end of her pink tongue dipped daintily into the cereal like she was worried she'd make a mess of her whiskers if she ate too fast. Each time the spoon emptied, I filled it again. Jedda took so long Lizzie was snoring before we were even halfway done.

On the third-last spoonful, the bundle inside my T-shirt began to move. It felt like Smooch was doing a tumble turn. One tumble turn became three.

'Carol!' I cried, trying not to panic. Lizzie sat bolt upright and tipped her head to the side. A volcano was erupting in my Santa belly. Perhaps Smooch didn't like me after all?

Carol was standing at the kitchen bench, rewrapping a bandage on an injured possum. She was at the tricky bit where you had to make sure it didn't all unravel, so she didn't look up when I called. 'What?' she said absently. Then, when she saw my stricken face, she added, 'First, calm down and then just stick your hand into your shirt and ease the pouch out. No need to panic.'

My mouth had gone completely dry. How would I know which end was up? What if he slipped out and cracked his head on the floor? I was supposed to be caring for him, not making things worse. So far I was a failure as a koala mother.

'Use both hands to unwrap the pouch. When you get to his body, hold him close. He might get a fright when he realises you're not me.'

I carefully unravelled the pouch until Smooch's grey fluffy ears and bright button eyes appeared. My hands were shaking but he wasn't the least bit worried that I wasn't Carol. He clawed his way out and clung onto my neck. Then he turned his head to look at Jedda's bowl.

Carol laughed. 'Greedy guts,' she said. 'He's got a whiff of Jedda's lunch. Stay there. I'll make him up a bottle.'

Jedda was getting fidgety. She wanted the last of her food and Smooch was making her wait. 'Here, give me the bowl,' said Carol when she came back from the kitchen. 'I'll finish up with Jedda and you feed Smooch. I think you're his favourite anyway.' She passed me a fresh warm bottle and I prised Smooch away from my neck. He guzzled down the whole lot and then snuggled into my lap for another snooze. I cuddled him into my arms and stroked his hairy ear with my thumb.

'You're my favourite too,' I whispered.

5. Lizzie

By the time strawberry season was over, Smooch had grown too heavy for the pouch around our bellies. He still liked nestling in my hair and having cuddles on my lap, but it wasn't quite the same as having him snuggled inside my shirt. Sometimes he would curl up next to Lizzie in the corner of Carol's couch and I'd have to wait for them both to wake up before I could go home.

But I didn't mind. The longer I spent away from home the better. Gran hadn't been the same since the letter from the bank. She moped about the place, obsessively flicking off light switches – to save electricity, she said – and complaining about all the carrots I fed Mickey. Worse still, she flinched every time the phone rang. It was always Uncle Malcolm anyway. Nag, nag, nag. The bank was getting impatient.

Not long after Christmas, Carol said Smooch was big and strong enough to move into the aviary in her shady backyard. He'd started stealing the other animals' food and nearly tipped Carol's bookcases over while practising how to climb. He was 16-months old now and as big as a football. Carol said it was time to prepare him for his release back into the wild.

I didn't think the move to the aviary was such a great idea. For a start it meant fewer cuddles. But worse, it meant Smooch could get hurt. He was safe inside the house with Carol, but outside, there were dogs and cats and even meddling kids. What if one of them broke into his cage? Carol said I should stop worrying, that Smooch would be just fine, and she kept me busy collecting leaves. Lots of leaves. In fact, Lizzie and I spent most of the summer holidays running between the creek at our farm and Carol's backyard, making sure Smooch had all the leaves he needed to make him strong enough for the wild.

One day, when the summer holidays were nearly over, I was lugging yet another stack of freshly cut eucalypt leaves over to Carol's, when I heard familiar voices giggling up ahead. I clutched the branches to my chest and jammed my face among the leaves. Lizzie's tail slunk between her legs. She didn't like the sound of the giggles either.

'You building an ark or what?' Kellee and Tahlia had planted themselves across the footpath in front of us. Their wet swimming pool hair and red icy pole lips made them look like saltwater crocodiles, ready to strike.

Go away, I prayed, squeezing my eyes shut. *Just leave me alone.*

'Bit extreme, don't you think? Carrying a whole tree? Most people wear hats to keep off the sun.' They laughed, a nasty, sneaky laugh that made my skin feel like maggots were wriggling over it. One of them, I'm not sure which, tugged at the branches. 'Hello? We can see you under there you know, bumpkin.'

I pulled back. They pulled harder, so I yanked the branches sideways. They came loose and I fell back, landing hard on my backside on the concrete. Lizzie scooted out of the way just in time. Leaves and branches were scattered all around me.

'Ha ha, serves you right, scarecrow. See ya at school,' laughed Tahlia, looping her arm through Kellee's and waltzing off down the path.

I watched them go, my elbows stinging, my eyes prickling with tears. Is that what they thought? That I was a scarecrow? With straw in my head instead of brains? A fat tear rolled down my cheek as I reached over to pick up the fallen branches. Maybe they were right. Maybe my head *was* filled with useless straw. It had been months since Gran had got the letter from the bank, and I hadn't managed to do anything about saving the farm.

A soft nose pushed gently against my face just as another tear threatened to plop onto the concrete. A rough tongue licked at my cheek. 'Lucky I've got you, hey Lizzie,' I murmured, pulling her to me and burying my face in her fur.

We'd already agreed on the place to release Smooch: down by the creek, near where we'd found him and his mum, almost nine months before. Carol checked with the other carers to make sure no other male koalas had taken over the area and by the time school went back for the year, Smooch was all ready to go.

'Couldn't I look after him?' I asked for the millionth time. 'We could build an enclosure off our verandah and I'd make sure he was safe and I . . .'

'No, he needs a bigger playground,' said Carol firmly. 'Anyway, why are you complaining? You'll be able to visit him *every* day, not just Saturdays.'

Smooch sat quietly in the cage as Gran, Carol,

Lizzie and I carried him to the creek. He wasn't frightened. Just curious.

'Here, we'll put him on this one,' said Carol, opening the cage and placing Smooch at the base of the tree. 'Koalas love tallowwoods.'

Gran rested her hand on my shoulder as we watched Smooch wrap his arms around the trunk, like he was hugging it. I sucked in a breath as he lifted his bottom, ready to climb. We waited, expecting him to go. But he didn't. Instead, he stopped and looked over, as if checking we were still there.

My eyes went all hot and runny. I dipped my face so Smooch couldn't see. 'Go on, Smooch,' I whispered. 'It's okay. Nothing will hurt you, I promise.'

Smooch turned back to the tree and Gran pulled me away. We stood with Carol and Lizzie at a distance and watched him climb until he got to a thick branch about halfway up. He pushed his bottom down into the 'V' between the branch and the trunk, clasping the tree with both hands. Then he looked down at us like he was making a decision, a very important decision. After a few seconds he blinked, and snuggled into his new home.

Lizzie and I checked on Smooch every day after that. We'd race down to the creek after school and would usually find him resting high up in his favourite tallowwood tree. I felt like singing every time I spotted his fuzzy grey face among the branches. It was so good to see him there. We'd saved him: Lizzie, Gran, Carol and me. Now it was our job to keep him safe. Not that Smooch seemed to care. He would turn his head and chew slowly while I grinned up at him, as if he wondered what all the fuss was about.

'I'm glad I've got you, Smooch,' I whispered one day. It was the day everyone but me received invitations to Kellee's birthday party. Even the *new*, new kids got one. Kellee made a point of telling me I wasn't invited – in front of everyone. Not that I wanted to go. I'd rather climb up in the tallowwood tree and spend the day with Smooch. 'We could eat leaves and have naps and stay safe, high in the treetops,' I told him. 'What do you think? Maybe I'll even stay. Never go to school. Never be called bumpkin or scarecrow again.' *And never see Gran's fingers tremble every time she opened the mail.* 'If only something would happen. If only everything would be okay.'

Not long before the start of the strawberry season, something did happen. Something horrible. And everything was definitely not okay.

Before heading out to the strawberry patch to help Gran, I'd raced into the house after school to change into my old jeans and favourite blue hoodie. Then I ducked into the kitchen to grab an apple.

That's when I saw Lizzie.

Curled up in her bed.

Like she was asleep.

I frowned. Lizzie always plastered me with muddy paw prints when I came home. Perhaps she hadn't heard me.

I stepped closer.

Her body was cold and her pale gums were stiff across her old yellowy teeth. My heart froze and my eyes welled. I knelt beside her and kissed her face over and over. But she didn't wake up. I stroked her head and scratched behind her ears. She still didn't move. I made myself let her go. I squeezed away my tears and stumbled outside. 'Gran!' I yelled. 'Come quick!'

Gran gave me a long hug when she saw Lizzie. 'At least she had a good life,' she murmured, her voice thick. 'She must have chased a thousand rabbits and she probably held the world record for eating strawberries.'

We sat beside Lizzie, Gran hugging me tight.

'Remember all the funny things she used to do?' said Gran. 'Like when she came home with a ring of red dirt around her neck? From sticking her head down too many rabbit holes? Remember?'

I sniffed. 'And when she stood on her back legs and spun around when Mum sang *Ring around the Rosie*? Like she was dancing?' I said, blowing my nose loudly.

'Yes, that's right. Before she got arthritis. Dear little thing. Come on, how about I make some hot drinks?'

Gran made tea and hot chocolate and we pulled the wicker chairs out onto the verandah. It had been Dad's favourite spot, even in winter when it was almost too cold to sit there. I wrapped my hands around my hot chocolate and breathed in the delicious chocolatey smell.

'How about we bury Lizzie under the tallow-wood tree, so she'll be near Smooch?' I suggested.

Gran sipped her tea. 'Mmm, maybe.'

A cold south-easterly was blowing up from the paddocks. I huddled into my hoodie as the wind whistled around the eaves of the verandah. I glanced over at Gran. Her wrinkles looked extra deep today. Her normally bright eyes were red and dull. I gulped down a sob. How would we survive without Lizzie?

'What about down by the kitchen steps?' I suggested. 'Next to Mum's lavender bushes?'

'Possibly.'

I frowned.

Gran wasn't listening. Her eyes were fixed on the neat rows of strawberry plants stretched out before us. Their green and white flowers were soft against the lines of silver plastic spread out around them. In a couple of weeks, those flowers would turn into thousands of bright red berries, juicy and sweet.

'I'm sorry, Rosie love,' she whispered eventually. 'Your Uncle Malcolm's right. I'm getting too old. I can't run this place by myself anymore. And now that Lizzie's gone . . .' Gran took a deep breath and sighed a long, heavy sigh. 'Rosie, we're going to have to sell the farm.'

I felt like someone had punched me in the stomach. Like the time I'd fallen off Mickey, Dad's old racehorse. Or when our goat, Sally, headbutted me in the guts. We were giving up? Just like that? No way. We grew the best strawberries in the whole of Redland Bay. I mean, our farm wasn't the biggest around, and anyone could easily drive past our place and not notice anything special . . .

But it *was* special.

Like Gran always said – things don't have to be big to be special.

'We'll see the strawberry season out at least,' said Gran, passing me a plate of gingernuts. I shook my head. I just didn't get it. Gran had lived on this farm her whole entire life. My dad and Uncle Malcolm had grown up here. I had practically grown up here too. She couldn't sell it – she just couldn't.

Gran dunked her gingernut into her tea. She looked old and tired. She took a feeble bite. 'The thing is, Uncle Malcolm says now's a good time to sell. There are plenty of developers interested in the area and he says they'll snap up a place like this. It's perfect for a housing estate, so they'll pay top dollar.'

When I thought about our farm getting chopped up into ugly townhouses, my heart turned into a tub of ice-cream left too long in the freezer – full of icicles and bitterly cold. So cold it hurt.

'What will happen to us if you sell?' I croaked.

I couldn't see Gran's face properly. She kept her head turned towards the strawberry plants. But I noticed her big brown hands trembling around her teacup. 'Things have a way of working out, love,' she said. 'It'll be for the best, you'll see. Uncle Malcolm's been very kind. We'll live with him in the city. He's got such a lovely big house, with a swimming pool and . . . I'm sure you'll like it there.'

The city? Where I'd have to wear city clothes and talk like city kids? And with Uncle Malcolm?

My ice-cream heart grew colder.

'But what about Mickey and Sally and the chooks? We can't leave them behind.'

'I'll talk to Mr Douglas. When his fruit farm sold, he took his sheep and chooks to his brother's cattle farm, out towards Toowoomba. When the time comes, maybe we can send Mickey and the others there.'

'But we can't move!' My voice had gone all high and whiny, like I'd sucked on a helium balloon. 'We can't leave Smooch. Who will look out for him if we go?'

6. Uncle Malcolm

Later that night, the phone rang. It echoed eerily through our cold dark house until Gran picked it up. I scrambled out of bed and crept into the hallway.

'I know. It's terribly sad, Malcolm dear,' Gran was saying. 'Yes, I know, poor little thing. Yes, I understand. Okay, yes, I see, well . . .'

I peeked into the kitchen. Gran had the phone to her ear and was staring out the darkened window. Her face was pinched and pale. 'Oh, really? That soon?' she said. 'What about the strawberry season? Okay, well, yes, I see . . .' She rubbed her forehead and leant her shoulder against the window. I wanted to run in and hug her, but I didn't. Instead I crept back to bed and curled up into a ball. If only Lizzie hadn't died. If only Mum and Dad were here. Why had they all gone and left Gran and me behind?

Uncle Malcolm showed up the following afternoon. He parked his fancy sports car in our drive and pulled out a laptop case before marching up to the house in his pointy black shoes. I practically choked on the smell of his sickly men's perfume as he passed me. But he didn't even give me a sideways glance. Instead, he stepped over the crates on the verandah, like he'd get an infection if he touched one. His shiny bald head jutting out of his black suit reminded me of a turtle with its head poking out from its shell. Only turtles didn't have fat ugly necks with bright purple ties knotted against them.

When Gran opened the front door, Uncle

Malcolm looked around and sniffed. Animals made his eyes itchy and his nose run, and if he touched one, he would break out in an angry red rash. I wished he would. Maybe then he'd go back to the city and leave us alone.

'You'll have to move the junk out of the yard,' he said as soon as he kissed Gran hello. Gran's lips thinned. I waited for her to tell him to stop talking smart. But her shoulders slumped and she kept her eyes down.

'Rosie love,' whispered Gran. 'You go on outside. Your Uncle Malcolm and I have some sorting out to do.'

I stomped around doing my chores that afternoon. I banged the door to the chicken pen, sending the chooks squawking and flapping. I clanged the buckets together on my way to feed Sally. I stirred Mickey's mash so hard I gave myself a blister. How could Gran do this? Didn't she know I wouldn't survive in the city?

As soon as my chores were done, I ran down the street to Carol's.

'Gran's doing it,' I puffed when Carol let me in. 'She's selling the farm. She's really selling the farm.'

'She is?' Carol's thin eyebrows folded inwards so fast they nearly crashed together. 'What's happened?'

My lips trembled and tears began to slide down my cheeks. 'It's Lizzie,' I managed to say. 'She died yesterday.'

Carol had been holding a basket of washing, but now she dropped it and wrapped her arms around me. 'Oh no,' she said. She pressed my wet face into her chest and stroked my hair. She smelt nice, not nice like lavender, like Mum, but nice like baby formula and breakfast cereal. She held me there for a long time and when she let me go, her T-shirt was damp with my tears. 'I'm so sorry. Lizzie was a very special dog. You'll miss her.'

I nodded. My voice wouldn't work.

'Tell you what, you can help me feed my new puggle. That'll cheer you up.'

She led me through to the kitchen and cleared a chair for me to sit down. I blew my nose and dried my tears while she bustled around making a bottle of formula. This wasn't a regular bottle – it was made from a small syringe with a long narrow teat on the end. When it was ready, she opened the little blue esky on the kitchen bench and pulled out the tiniest grey creature I'd ever seen. When she passed him to me, he lay curled up in a ball in the palm of my hand with his pink claws sticking out. His long pointy nose sniffed the air.

'What is he?' I whispered.

'He's a baby echidna,' said Carol, passing me the bottle. 'He's about a month and a half old. You just squeeze drops of milk onto your hand and he'll suck it up from there. '

For a moment I forgot about Lizzie. I forgot about Gran and Uncle Malcolm. I was too busy feeding the puggle. He snuffled at his milk like a tiny elephant. When he finished, he started hiccupping so violently I was scared I would drop him, so I passed him to Carol.

'We have to move to the city,' I said. 'I won't be able to see you or Smooch or . . .' I swallowed the lump rising in my throat.

Carol shook her head sadly as she rubbed the puggle's belly with her fingers. 'That's too bad. It's going to be tough. But there *is* a positive side. Did you know they sell chocolate pizza in the city?'

'I don't like pizza.'

'Okay, no pizza. There are movies. All kids like movies. And ice skating and . . .'

I frowned. 'I don't want to go ice skating.'

'Hey, give yourself a break. You'll love it. You'll be too busy to worry about me and my babies. And Smooch will be just fine without you.'

'No! No, he won't! He won't be fine! Smooch needs me. I'm the one who looks after him. I'm the one who—'

The puggle in Carol's hand started at my loud voice and almost tumbled to the floor. Carol cupped her hands to stop him from falling. 'Okay, okay, calm down. When do you go? Is it soon?'

'Well, the farm's not sold yet,' I mumbled. 'I mean, anything could happen . . .'

An ugly yellow FOR SALE sign appeared at our gate the very next week. Big red letters plastered across it screamed, 'Exciting New Development Opportunity!' Exciting? It wasn't the least bit exciting. I wanted to puke every time I saw the sign. Surveyors wearing fluoro jackets and business men in black tromped all over our farm, with maps and measuring tapes and no concerns for Gran or Sally or Mickey or me. They were only interested in one thing: the land. Our street turned into a carpark with all the people coming and going, and I expected Gran to tell me to pack my bags any day. But she didn't. People came and people went. For weeks. Heads nodded. Mobiles rang. When no SOLD sign appeared, hope trickled into my heart.

The pickers arrived in May to pick the red juicy strawberries. The first of the last juicy red strawberries. I limped through second term, my books open but my mind a million miles away. Maybe we wouldn't sell? Maybe no-one had the money? Perhaps now Gran would tell Uncle Malcolm to get lost? She knew I could never live in the city. Especially not with a nagging, shouting uncle who was allergic to everything.

Term three came and went and, as the weather warmed up, the strawberries started to dwindle. But despite all my hopes, the interest in our farm did not. Gran said we'd had some very promising offers, but so far none of them had followed through. I refused to listen when she tried to tell me the details. I preferred to imagine it wasn't going to happen at all.

One day in the first week of term four, our teacher, Mrs Glover, began talking in her important-piece-of-information voice. Mrs Glover had been teaching at my school for 1,000 years and everyone knew she was the toughest teacher around.

'Everyone clear? A one-minute PowerPoint presentation. You have six weeks, so you'll need to get organised.' She squeezed through the middle row of desks, pushing rulers and pencil cases out of her way. 'This is the main assessment piece for the term, so I expect you to give it your best. Absolutely no extensions.'

A one-minute presentation? I'd been so busy worrying about the farm that I missed what it should be about. I searched the whiteboard for clues.

Due: week seven. A persuasive presentation on an endangered native animal. Include what they eat, where they live and tell us why we should save them.

Mrs Glover's writing was so neat it looked like one of the fonts in Microsoft Word.

I copied down the instructions, trying not to panic. Public speaking always made me sick. But public speaking in front of Kellee and Tahlia would be a death sentence.

7. Sold

One night a few weeks later, the kitchen smelt of lamb roast. We hardly ever had roasts. Gran usually saved them for birthdays and super special occasions.

'Good news,' said Gran when I asked her what we were celebrating.

My heart soared. 'We're keeping the farm?'

Gran didn't answer.

'We've paid off all the bills?'

Gran still didn't answer. Instead she asked me to set the table for three while she piled crispy roast potatoes and juicy slices of lamb onto the plates and sloshed gravy over the lot. Why wasn't she talking to me? Was I invisible or something?

'Gran!' I demanded. '*Why* are we having a roast?'

'I was going to wait for Uncle Malcolm. He'll be here any minute.' She glanced out the dark window.

'Gran!'

She rubbed her eyes and then clapped her hands together like it was exciting news. But she didn't look excited. 'Rosie . . . we've sold the farm. I didn't say anything earlier because we've been waiting for the approvals. But I found out today. We've sold. And at a great price. A *fantastic* price.'

I crossed my arms. Her voice was funny and she was talking too quickly. And she didn't look at me when she spoke. 'Uncle Malcolm will be here shortly,' she continued. 'He's been negotiating all day.' She smiled, but it wasn't a real smile. Not a crinkly eyes smile.

I wanted to scream. NO! We couldn't sell! NO! NO! NO!

'We CAN'T move!' I shouted. 'Not now! What about Carol and Smooch and . . . ?'

Gran wasn't listening. She seemed more interested in poking at the pieces of lamb on our plates.

'NO!' I shouted. 'I WON'T leave the farm! I hate the city. I hate Uncle Malcolm. I HATE city kids.' Hot tears welled in my eyes. I ran out of the kitchen and into my room. How could Uncle Malcolm do this to us? Why didn't Gran stand up to him? We would have gotten the money from somewhere.

I lay on my bed, wishing I hadn't left Brownie at Carol's. I missed having someone to cuddle. I waited until I heard Uncle Malcolm's car pull up in the driveway, and made sure he went into the kitchen with Gran before creeping down to Gran's room. I slid open her bedside drawer. Nestled towards the back, among her tubes of hand cream and faded birthday cards, was Mum's old wheat pack. It smelt of lavender and of Mum. She used to heat it for me when I got sick and then cuddle beside me in bed, reading me stories until I fell asleep.

I curled up on Gran's bed and put the wheat pack against my stomach. It weighed about the same as Smooch when he was still in Carol's pouch. Mum wasn't there to read me stories, and the pack wasn't warm like Smooch, or soft and tickly, but it made me feel better. At least Smooch would be okay. He was safe – high up in his tallowwood tree.

Sometime later I heard footsteps at the door. 'Come on, Rosie love,' said Gran softly. 'Come and give your old gran a hand.' Something about the way she said it made me swallow my tears. It wasn't her fault we had to sell the farm.

The cold lino floor and the draught from the back door made the kitchen the coldest room in the house. The sink sat below a big window that overlooked the farm. At night our reflections watched eerily over us when we stood at the sink and did the washing up.

'Gran,' I said when I finally found my voice. 'What will happen to me in the city? I'm not like city kids. They think I'm weird and . . . I won't have any friends.'

Gran stopped scrubbing the roasting dish. She straightened and looked me in the eye for the first time all night. 'Rosie dear,' she said, 'if there's something I've learnt in the last few weeks, it's that everything changes. Just like the wind.'

'But what if you don't want it to change? What if—?'

'You can't control the wind, love.' She returned to the dish. 'You have to be brave and put up your sails. No point in standing firm – you'll only capsize.'

I didn't answer and we finished the washing up in silence.

'Come on, chin up,' said Gran, pulling out the plug. 'Tell me about school. What are you working on?'

I swallowed hard and swiped angrily at my nose. 'We have to do a persuasive PowerPoint,' I mumbled. 'It's due in two weeks.'

'You haven't told me about this,' said Gran. 'A power what?'

'It's a stupid one-minute presentation. One whole minute – in front of the entire class.'

'On what?' asked Gran.

'We have to choose an endangered Australian animal and—'

'Bah! Rosie Nunn, you could talk about animals till you were blue in the face. What animal have you chosen?'

'I'm doing a koala. You know, 'cause of Smooch,' I said. 'I'll need heaps of information and loads of pictures too.'

'Smooch. Great idea,' she said. 'Isn't it, Malcolm?'

Uncle Malcolm had come into the kitchen without me hearing. I didn't realise he was still here. Now he peered at me over his reading glasses, like I was a pesky toad.

'Smooch?' he said, pulling off his glasses and rubbing at his eyes. 'Who or what is Smooch?'

Gran gave me an encouraging smile and said, 'Tell him, Rosie.'

I fiddled with the damp tea towel in my hand. 'It's . . . about a . . . koala. I—'

'A koala? You haven't got a koala in the house, have you?' Uncle Malcolm looked anxiously over my shoulder. 'You know how allergic . . .'

'Oh for goodness sake!' snapped Gran. 'She's talking about the koala down by the creek.' Her lips were tight. 'Remember how you and David used to love the creek when you were kids? Rosie saved a koala down there last year. His name is Smooch and she's going to write about him for her science project.'

Uncle Malcolm snorted. 'Well, good luck with that,' he said. 'You'd better hop to it. The contractors will be here soon. Can't imagine the bulldozers will care two hoots about your Hooch, or Pooch, or whatever its name is.'

'Smooch,' I mumbled. Then a little more loudly, 'What do you mean *bulldozers*?'

Uncle Malcolm laughed. 'Bulldozers. They'll pull down the lot. No trees will be left standing, koala or no koala.'

My mouth fell open. I stared at Uncle Malcolm in disbelief. 'They can't do that,' I said. 'Koalas are native Australian animals. We saved Smooch when his mum died. I promised I'd look after him.' I glanced at Gran. She was clutching the back of a kitchen chair. Her eyes were wide and dark.

'Surely not?' she said, pulling out the chair and sinking into it. 'All the trees?'

'It's too late now!' said Uncle Malcolm, his voice rising. 'The council's given the developers the full go-ahead and believe me, judging from the other developments around here, *all* the trees will go.'

8. Missing

The next morning, I zoomed over to Carol's place as soon as I was dressed. I had to find out the rules for clearing koala trees. Uncle Malcolm couldn't possibly be right.

'Haven't you got school this morning?' asked Carol after she opened the door. She was holding a red and green lorikeet wrapped in an old towel, so she beckoned me in with her elbows. 'What's up?'

I followed her into the kitchen. 'You have to help. They're going to clear all of Smooch's trees!'

'Wait,' said Carol, putting the lorikeet in a small

cage perched on the bench. She latched the door shut and turned to give me her full attention. 'Who's going to clear all of whose trees?'

'The developers. The ones who bought our farm. They can't do that, can they? Isn't it against the law?'

Carol sat down on one of the kitchen chairs and nodded gravely to the chair beside her. 'Here's the thing,' she said. 'At the moment, koalas are protected, but not their trees. If the trees at your creek haven't been noted as "protected", then the developers *can* knock them down. It's not against the law.'

'But what do you mean by "protected"?'

'It's complicated. If there's a koala in a tree when the council checks on the property, it will be marked "protected". That means the tree can't be knocked down. But if there is no koala when they come out to do their inspection, the developers can go ahead.'

I breathed a big sigh of relief. 'Well, that's okay then. They'll see Smooch when they come. The trees will be marked and the developers won't be able to bulldoze them. Huh! Wait till I tell Uncle Malcolm!' I stood up to go.

'Mmm, well, it's not as simple as that. There's a lot of rules and . . . '

'What rules?'

'Too many to remember. Hop on my computer and take a look.'

Carol's computer whizzed and whirred as I typed 'koala' into the search engine. There was heaps of information, ranging from furry marsupial fact sheets to a rock band called The Rocking Koalas. My eyes darted to Carol's clock. It was nearly 8.15.

I scrolled down one of the pages to a heading that said: *Is There a Koala in Danger Near You?* Three pictures came up across the top of the page. The first showed a bulldozer ramming a tree. A koala clung desperately to a spindly branch as the tree swayed sideways. The second picture showed a block of land totally cleared of trees and bushes. The red soil was jagged with broken branches and roots. The third showed a suburban street not unlike the new streets in our neighbourhood. It was lined with brand-new houses, smart-green lawns and plastic-looking hedges. It was all so neat and tidy. And there was not a gum tree in sight.

Icicles began to shatter inside my ice-cream heart. Was this what Uncle Malcolm meant? Would this be our farm in a few weeks' time? I scanned down the page. Below the pictures was a heading: *What Can You Do?* The suggestions included writing letters to your local councillors, to the newspapers, to your local Member of Parliament and to the Minister for the Environment in your state. There was even a sample letter, which I quickly printed.

'What do you think?' I asked Carol when I showed it to her.

'I think you should do it,' she said, wiping her hands on her jeans to take the letter from me. She gave it a quick once over and handed it back. 'Stand up for what you believe in and write to everybody, I say. Do you need some addresses?'

I began writing straight after school that afternoon. I wrote and wrote and wrote until my fingers cramped. I wrote a letter to our local councillor, one to our local Member of Parliament, to the Queensland Minister for the Environment and, just to be on the safe side, to Australia's Environment Minister in Canberra. Carol had also given me the addresses for two local papers as well as the biggest newspaper in Brisbane. I wrote to them all. I told them about Smooch, explaining that the worst thing we could do was let developers bulldoze his trees. I told them it was no good catching Smooch and taking him somewhere else. He'd only try to get back home and end up being killed by a car or a dog along the way. I finished off the letters asking if they wanted to come and see the creek and Smooch for themselves. I knew they'd understand if they saw him. I ended by saying they'd have to hurry. The developers would be here any day. Then I signed each letter: *Yours sincerely, Rose Nunn.*

I snuck some envelopes and stamps from Gran's writing bureau and raced to the red postbox at the end of our street. I held my letters up to the slot, took a deep breath and then closed my eyes. 'Please help Smooch,' I begged. Then I opened my eyes and shoved in the letters.

It was getting dark by the time I got back home. I threw off my school dress and tugged on my jeans and blue hoodie before racing down to the creek. I wanted to tell Smooch what I'd done. He had to know I wouldn't let the developers cut down his trees.

My eyes swept the treetops. Smooch wasn't in his favourite tallowwood. Or the paperbark next to it. Or the scribbly gum two trees over. I brushed past the long grasses with their sticky seed heads and swiped a couple of fallen branches out of my way. I craned my neck. Still nothing. It smelt like a deep dark forest down here. Two black crows cawed at me from the flaking paperbark trees. A noisy miner tweeted from high up in the canopy. Dad had known the call of every single bird at our creek. I bet he would've known where Smooch was.

I squinted harder into the canopy. It suddenly seemed eerily quiet. Mysteriously still. My feet squelched in the mud. My breath echoed in my ears.

All the trees were empty.

Smooch wasn't in *any* of them.

There was something else though. Something orange – over on the far bank. I scrambled across the creek on a fallen scribbly log. My heart flipped. An ugly orange stake was wedged like a flagpole in the mud. Another one stood a few metres further along. And another. I counted eighteen orange stakes in all. They stood like an intruding army of silent soldiers in the bush.

What were they for? And where was Smooch?

9. Growing Up

I hurried back across the log and ran all the way up to the house. I had to find Gran.

I found her in the kitchen, stirring a pot of soup on the stove.

'Smooch is gone!' I spluttered, trying not to cry.

Gran looked small and frail stirring the big pot. She was staring into it, like the swirling soup had hypnotised her.

I tried a little more loudly. 'Gran!'

She looked up, startled. 'Rosie! There you are. Sorry love, I was miles away. Ready for dinner?'

'Gran, Smooch is missing! There are orange stakes down the creek, they've scared Smooch off, and—'

'Slow down, Rosie,' sighed Gran, setting out the bowls.

'Smooch is *missing*. They won't know that a koala lives at the creek! They'll chop down all the trees.'

Gran pushed a strand of hair from her eyes. 'Rosie love,' she murmured. 'Smooch is a big boy now, all grown up, just like you. I'm sure he's not missing. He's probably just gone for a little explore. Now, do me a favour and lay the table.'

I could hardly eat my soup. Gran wouldn't hear any more about Smooch. She said she had enough to worry about trying to sell the farm machinery and cleaning out the sheds without adding a missing koala to the list. She didn't want to hear about koala websites or letters or laws about koala trees. Apparently there was some hiccup with the sale contract that was making Uncle Malcolm extra cranky and Gran drifted off to bed as soon as the dishes were done.

I hoped the hiccup was a big one. A giant one. Perhaps it would mean we wouldn't have to sell the farm.

On the way to school the next day, I stopped in at Carol's. I had to tell her that Smooch was missing. I found her in the back garden, feeding the wild rosellas.

'Don't worry,' she said as she dug into the bin of bird feed. 'He'll be back.' Seeds flicked everywhere as about 20 noisy rosellas squawked and flapped over the dish. 'Maybe he's just growing up?'

There were those two words again. Growing up. Why did everybody keep talking about growing up? A black and white butterfly flittered past. I frowned. Butterflies. Grown-up caterpillars. I stuck my hands in my pockets. Why was everything growing up?

'Will he come back?' I said, my voice growlier than I meant it to be.

'Course he will,' said Carol, sealing the lid on the feed bin. 'Male koalas wander all the time.

Smooch isn't old enough to mate yet, but he's probably gone off to check out all the pretty girls in the neighbourhood. Don't worry about it. He won't be too far away.'

Part of me was cross that Smooch was growing up, but a bigger part of me was relieved that he wasn't hurt. Maybe, while he was wandering, he'd find a safer place to live.

'But what about the orange stakes?' I asked. 'They're everywhere at the creek. Does that mean the council's been? When Smooch wasn't around? Because then they won't have marked his trees.'

Carol looked sadly around the garden. 'Yes. The orange stakes will be surveyor's pegs, marking out the land for development. Which means the council would definitely have already been through.' She slapped a mosquito trying to feast on her arm. 'We could have a problem.'

'What about my letters?' I insisted. 'I mean, they'll help, won't they? I wrote to everybody the website suggested. Surely someone will . . .'

'Maybe not, Rose. People often have bigger things to worry about than koalas. We'll have to think of something else. Something more convincing. Something impressive. Any ideas?'

I chewed the inside of my cheek. 'What about a fundraiser?' I suggested. 'We have silly socks days and pyjama days at my school. We could have one for Smooch and use the money to buy the creek back.'

Carol shook her head. 'No, too late for that. And we'd need a lot of socks! We need something to raise awareness about the koalas and their trees.'

'Like a protest march? We could start at the farm gate and march into town, with banners and loudspeakers and—'

'Maybe not a protest march. Not yet. There has to be something else we can try first.'

We decided we'd have a better think over the weekend. After saying goodbye to Carol, I ran all the way to school. But it was no use. I was late. The rest of the class was already copying notes from the interactive whiteboard. Mrs Glover didn't turn around when I walked in.

I squeezed behind my desk and ruled up a new page in my book.

'Miss Nunn?' said Mrs Glover in her sharp don't-mess-with-me voice. 'You have a note, I presume?'

I sat still, hoping she'd get distracted.

'Miss Nunn. A late note?'

I shook my head.

'This is the second time you've been late this term. I hope it's not becoming a habit.'

I wanted to tell her that I was never late on purpose. Only if Mickey twisted his rug, or if Sally got out and I had to chase her back into her yard. It wasn't my fault if I was worried about Smooch. Surely she'd understand? This was an emergency.

But I kept my mouth shut. I knew there was no point arguing with Mrs Glover.

The morning lesson was about petitions made to the Queensland Parliament. Mrs Glover handed out a pile of examples and asked us to work in groups. She stopped beside me and pointed to Kellee and Tahlia. 'You can work with the girls at the back today, Rose,' she said. 'There are some tricky words to watch out for in this worksheet. Girls, give Rose a hand, please.'

Kellee said, 'Oh, great!' And Tahlia groaned.

I stared grimly at my desk. *Anybody but them.*

Mrs Glover gave a petition to Tahlia, and clicked her fingers impatiently at me. 'Snap, snap, Rose. We haven't got all day,' she said curtly.

I stood and dragged my feet to the back of the room.

'Snap, snap, bumpkin,' giggled Kellee. She and Tahlia shuffled their chairs together as I fumbled into my seat. I gripped my pencil and rubber for moral support.

'What's the matter, scarecrow? Too much straw for breakfast?' sniggered Tahlia.

I pretended to study the petition. It didn't look that different to the letters I'd written to the newspapers and politicians. Only with a heap more signatures.

Tahlia reached over and snatched the petition away. 'As if you'd know, hay brain,' she hissed, flicking my pencil to the floor. She and Kellee turned their backs to me and bent over the worksheet. I bit my lip. Like I really cared about some old petition. Especially when koalas were being bulldozed in Redland Bay.

That got me thinking.

'Mrs Glover,' I asked when she came over. 'Could *anyone* write a petition? I mean, even if they're not someone important?'

She straightened up and peered at me over her glasses. 'Yes, of course. Isn't that what today's lesson has been all about?'

Kellee and Tahlia curled their lips.

Mrs Glover didn't notice. 'These are ordinary people putting forward petitions, trying to make a difference about things that really matter to them.'

'So, if *I* sent a petition about something really important, even *I* could make a difference? The people in Canberra would listen to my petition?'

Mrs Glover tapped her finger thoughtfully against her cheek. 'Mmm,' she said. 'Now that all depends on what the petition is requesting. If it's asking for a change in things like taxes or employment, then, yes, you'd send it to Canberra. But if it's to do with the environment or school, then you'd send it to your local State Member of Parliament. They would listen and lodge it, but they wouldn't necessarily have to *agree* to *do* whatever it is you want.' She folded her arms. 'Why? What do you want to change, Rose?'

Kellee nudged Tahlia's leg with her pencil. She did it just under the desk where Mrs Glover couldn't see. But I saw. I decided not to tell Mrs Glover about my idea.

I would write a petition for Smooch. A petition to save koala trees. I would ask everyone to sign it and I'd send it straight to my local state member. If I made sure it was good enough, they might even show it to the premier.

I ducked into the library at lunchtime and nabbed one of the computers before anyone else.

Instead of working on my PowerPoint, I typed up a petition asking for the protection of koala trees and made a whole heap of lines for people to sign their names. I checked the spelling four times and printed it off. For the first time in weeks, I felt a little sparkle of hope. I couldn't wait to fill the petition with signatures. Surely now Smooch would be saved.

10. Late Again

I filled up five pages of my petition with signatures, including one from Craig the vet, one from the school librarian, one from the lollipop lady, and even one from my principal. I didn't ask Mrs Glover. She didn't seem the animal type. When everyone I knew had signed it, I sent it off to the Member for Cleveland and asked him to please show the premier.

The petition kept me pretty busy, which was good because it stopped me worrying about Smooch. Every day I searched all the trees on the way to school and on the way home, but he wasn't in any of them.

The orange stakes were still down the creek. There were even some up near the yards now. People in fluoro jackets tromped all over our paddocks just about every day, but mostly they stayed away from the house.

'How much longer till we have to . . . you know . . . ?' I asked Gran late one afternoon. We were sitting on the verandah, eating homemade scones, and I didn't want to ruin the moment by saying the word 'move'.

'Not quite yet,' said Gran. 'There's still that hiccup with the contract. They're letting us stay on until they sort it out.'

My brain fizzled with joy. There was still a hiccup? Was it because of my letters after all? Or the petition? Maybe they'd already passed a law preventing the developers from chopping down Smooch's trees. Or maybe the developers had just changed their minds. Perhaps, because I'd been brave and spoken up, they'd decided to leave us alone.

'So we won't have to live with Uncle Malcolm?' I said, sitting a little straighter.

'No love. Well, yes, but not for the time being. We can wait until they sort things out.'

'Oh,' I said, sinking back into my chair. Then I jolted upright again. 'But that means there's still time to save Smooch's trees. There's got to be something else we can do.'

'No, I don't think there's anything else, Rosie,' said Gran. 'Mrs Henry up the road tried to save a few scribbly gums when her land was sold, and although the developers nodded their heads, they bulldozed them anyway.'

I took a bite of scone but even though it was smothered in delicious strawberry jam, thinking about bulldozers made the dough all sticky in my mouth.

'I understand you're upset about us selling the farm, Rosie, but your Uncle Malcolm's right. It really is for the best. We're not getting anywhere near the money we used to for strawberries and I'm not getting any younger.'

'It's not that,' I huffed. 'I know we have to sell the farm and everything. I just don't want them to bulldoze *all* the trees.'

I'd explained all the stuff I'd read on the koala websites to her before but she never seemed to listen. It was like she'd already given up on the farm and didn't want to fight.

I was never going to give up.

'Maybe it's time for a protest march,' I suggested. 'They'd have to listen then, wouldn't they?'

'Maybe,' said Gran, taking another sip of tea. And then, not sounding very convinced, 'You could try.'

I woke the next morning with Gran shaking my arm. 'Rosie!' she puffed breathlessly. 'You've slept in. I've fed the animals, but you'd better skedaddle. You'll be late for school.'

My alarm hadn't gone off! I dived out of bed and raced to school without breakfast. I would have made it too, if only I hadn't seen a white and grey lump on the side of the road. I stopped dead. Smooch?

A car roared past, blaring its horn. The lump didn't move. I wanted to shout, 'Get away, quick!' as I started running towards it. When I was about a metre away, I froze. What if it *was* Smooch? All bloodied and ripped? I stepped backwards. A sudden gust of wind flicked a strand of hair across my face. I pushed it away. The same gust caught the white and grey thing from where it lay. It flapped and rose and fluttered away. It wasn't Smooch. It was just a plastic bag!

I exhaled and tried to settle my pounding heart. Maybe this time it hadn't been him but what about next time? I sank to the curb and held my head in my hands. That bag was a sign. A sign that if I didn't do something, Smooch would end up dead on the side of the road. He needed me to help save him. If I didn't, who would?

I strode off to school, determined to talk to Mrs Glover about a protest march. I stepped into the classroom, my head held high. All eyes turned to me. I was late – again – but today would be okay. I had a good excuse. I steeled myself for a lecture and made my way to my desk.

But then I stopped. Tahlia was standing up the front holding a set of sharp teeth. Behind her, pictures of fierce Tasmanian devils flashed across the interactive whiteboard. I glanced around the room. One girl had a model of a large crab-looking thing sitting on her desk and another held a jar with something green and slimy cowering inside it.

Of course – presentation day! The PowerPoints! Mrs Glover waved an impatient hand at me and I slunk into my chair. I had only three measly slides on my USB and not a single prop. If only I hadn't spent so much time researching ways to save Smooch, I might have been more prepared.

I did a quick calculation. Mrs Glover liked doing things alphabetically and Tahlia's surname was Baker. There were 20 students on the roll between Baker and Nunn. Allowing one minute of talking per student and two minutes of questions plus the usual feet-dragging turn-around time. It would take five minutes for each person. Twenty people at five minutes apiece meant at least one hour and 40 minutes before Mrs Glover would call on me. It was now 9.15. We started sport at 12 and there was morning tea in between. If I was lucky, I might just slip through without doing my presentation.

I let out a deep breath and forced myself to concentrate on the whiteboard. Tahlia had included background music in her presentation and had all sorts of facts and figures. I shrank into my chair. My PowerPoint needed lots of work.

Tahlia finished her talk by asking for questions. I was pleased to see three hands shoot up. The more time we wasted the better. She answered each question perfectly and Mrs Glover smiled. She told us that Tahlia had delivered *exactly* the type of PowerPoint she'd been looking for and that she hoped she could expect the same quality from everyone in the class. There was some uncomfortable shuffling around the room.

Mrs Glover jotted down some notes in her mark book and then her eyes panned the room. I waited for her to call up Kellee. Her surname was Caper, and she was next on the roll after Tahlia. She even started gathering her notes and pushing back her chair.

I flinched when I heard my name.

'Miss Nunn!' repeated Mrs Glover. 'Let's hope your presentation was of higher priority than getting to school on time today . . . mmm?'

I gulped. Me? Now? I heard a snort from the back of the room. Tahlia and Kellee were waiting like red-bellied black snakes to strike. I had to think of an excuse. Quickly.

'I . . . um . . . we had a computer glitch at home,' I stuttered. 'Our hard drive . . . um . . . froze . . .'

'You don't even have a computer,' sneered Tahlia. A chorus of teehees trilled from the back. My face burnt.

'Sorry, Mrs Glover,' I mumbled. 'Can I do mine tomorrow? I . . . I only need a few more pictures and then I'll be ready.'

Mrs Glover tapped her pen on her hand. Twenty-six faces stared up at her in anticipation.

I was hopeless at public speaking. And everyone knew it. I hung my head low. *Please don't make me go. Please.*

Mrs Glover cleared her throat. 'If you remember, Miss Nunn, I said no extensions. Do you remember me saying that? Class?'

Everyone murmured a nervous yes. I was sure I wasn't the only person who hadn't finished their slides.

'Up you get, young lady. Let's see what you've got.'

My hands shook as I rummaged through my pencil case. I hoped I couldn't find my USB, but there it was, right on the top. I handed it to Mrs Glover. She plugged it into her laptop as I positioned myself in front of the whiteboard. My knees wobbled like crazy.

I twisted my hands together. 'Good morning, class. Good morning, Mrs Glover.' My eyes stayed glued to my shoes. I'd wound black tape over the toe to cover a large scruffy hole at the beginning of the year so Gran wouldn't have to buy me a new pair. The tape had been peeling off all term. I'd need to . . . *This isn't about shoes. Focus, focus, breathe.*

It felt like an hour passed. Every time I opened my mouth a nervous giggle escaped instead of my proper voice.

'There's nothing funny about it, Rose. We're waiting.'

'My presentation today is about the . . . um . . . the . . . um . . . the endangered Australian animal, the . . . um . . . the koala.' I reached for the remote to click on my first slide. My palm was hot and sweaty. The remote slipped and rattled noisily to the floor. I dived under the nearest desk to retrieve it.

'But the koala isn't endangered,' said someone at the back of the room. It sounded like Kellee. I stayed under the desk longer than I needed to. Maybe Mrs Glover would feel sorry for me and let me go sit down.

'Yeah. There are thousands of koalas, aren't there?' said someone else. 'You can't do a presentation on them.'

My fingers curled around the remote. Koalas *were* endangered. They were dying all around the place. Hadn't the websites said that? I couldn't make myself stand back up. What if I'd got it all wrong?

'That's enough, class. Let Rose continue. Rose, out of there. Keep going, please.'

I crawled out from under the desk and pushed my hair from my eyes. *Breathe, breathe.* Click. My first slide was a photo of Smooch, high up in his tallowwood tree. 'This is a typical . . . um . . . a typical koala,' I muttered, staring at my shoes. 'They eat gumleaves.'

'Duh!' said Kellee. I waited for her to say something about *me* eating gumleaves, but I looked up to see Mrs Glover giving her a glare.

I started again. 'They eat gumleaves. They have to chew them very slowly because um . . . because . . .' I puffed out my cheeks. Stupid idea. When I let the air out, it made a ridiculous popping sound. Mrs Glover shook her head. *Think, think.* Why *did* they chew slowly? It had something to do with digestion. But I couldn't remember. My brain had frozen. 'Um . . . they chew slowly because . . .'

I gave up. I clicked on the next slide. It was the picture I'd found of the koala clinging to the only tree in a totally cleared development site. The room went silent. No fiddling or wriggling. Just silence. All eyes facing me. I was supposed to say that koala numbers were dropping fast, but that picture made my chest heave and I had to choke down a sob. I couldn't trust my voice to utter another word. I was terrified I would cry.

'Rose?' said Mrs Glover, coming over to me. Her voice was surprisingly kind. 'Rose, have you any more slides?'

I nodded but didn't trust myself to speak. My eyes stung with tears.

'Okay, well, I think that's probably enough for today. How about you practise when you get home tonight and be ready to try again first thing tomorrow?'

I nodded again.

'Right, let's have Kellee up next. Kellee, are you ready?'

The rest of the day was a blur. All I remembered was someone talking about weird short-nosed sea snakes, which made everyone squeal, and Kellee giving an amazing presentation on the hairy-nosed wombat. I vowed to practise my talk a million times before tomorrow. I'd practise in front of Gran and maybe even Carol and I'd make sure I was super-prepared to present the next morning.

But the next morning, my PowerPoint presentation was the last thing on my mind.

11. Bulldozers

I woke up to the sound of Mickey whinnying. A high-pitched, terrified whinny. Over and over again. I raced outside in my pyjamas. He was galloping back and forth across his paddock, his nostrils wide. His tail was held high and his neck was arched. His body was slick with sweat. I vaulted off the verandah and ran to his fence.

'Mickey!' I yelled. 'Mickey!'

He stopped and swivelled in my direction, ears straining and nostrils quivering. Finally, his tail dropped and he cantered over to me. He nuzzled my outstretched palm for carrots, but when he realised I didn't have any, he took off. His tail streamed behind him as he galloped.

I scanned the strawberry patches first. What was he so upset about? Was he spooked by something flapping in the breeze? Like a piece of silver plastic broken free from under the strawberry plants and caught around a fence post? No. It had to be more than that. Mickey was going crazy. I turned to check the rest of the farm. That's when I saw it. I clamped my hands to my head. A huge orange bulldozer was winding its way towards the creek!

I didn't care about being in my pyjamas and started running. I ran through Mickey's paddock and ducked under the fence. My bare feet pounded the damp grass.

The bulldozer roared forwards through the trees. Saplings split and cracked against its hard metal blade. The air smelt of eucalyptus and diesel. I sprinted up to the huge machine and leapt up and down beside the cab. 'Stop!' I yelled. 'You have to stop!' The driver was so high above me he didn't see me at first. He was staring straight ahead as though knocking down trees was the most boring job on earth. I waved my arms frantically above my head. I yelled and jumped some more. 'Stop! Slow down!'

Eventually, the driver saw me and slowed the bulldozer down. When it fully stopped, the window popped open and a yellow helmet appeared. The driver leant out and looked down at me with surprise. 'What on earth . . . ?' he shouted above the roar of the engine.

'You can't come through here. It's private property!' I shouted.

He turned the engine off and swung open the door. He pulled a pile of papers from the dashboard and flicked through them with thick, hairy hands. 'Don't say that here, sweetheart,' he said. 'Says it's the property of Hall and Young. Got orders to flatten the lot. All 'cept the house and yards. I'd stand clear if I was you.' He threw the papers down onto the seat beside him and reached to close the door.

'No!' I screamed. But the driver shook his head and I tripped backwards as the bulldozer roared back to life. The caterpillar tyres rolled forwards and the enormous orange monster lurched towards the trees. My heart lurched with it. I had to do *something*! *Anything*!

There was only one thing to do. Before I could change my mind, I ran to Smooch's tallowwood tree. I hugged my arms around it, clasping the trunk like a sinking life raft in the ocean. I squeezed my eyes shut. The only way I could stop myself from running away was to imagine I was riding Mickey, high above the clouds. His chestnut coat glistened like the Melbourne Cup favourite Dad had hoped he would be. We flew in perfect silence, he and I, his mane drifting like silk behind us.

'I said – MOVE!'

Mickey and I crashed to the ground. The driver was stomping across the dewy grass towards me. Now that the engine had stopped, I could hear Mickey, still whinnying in his paddock.

I held my breath. The driver was getting closer.

What was he going to do to me? His arms were so strong and muscly. They looked more like legs than arms. They could crush a girl like me in seconds . . .

A strange sound came from high up in the tree. The driver stopped and looked up. The sound came again. A mixture of a pig's grunt and cow's bellow. With my arms still around the trunk, I tipped my head up too. A familiar grey shape sat high in the canopy of the tallowwood tree.

Smooch!

My heart swooped. He was alive! He was actually alive! Carol must have been right – he'd just gone walkabout and now here he was, as if nothing had happened!

I grinned. It was great to see him.

But his timing couldn't have been worse.

The driver started towards me again. He was close enough for me to smell his sweat. My stomach squirmed. I prepared for the worst. Suddenly, a loud voice shouted, 'Don't take another step. If you lay a hand on my granddaughter . . .'

Gran was wearing her usual green overalls, the ones with strawberry stains down the front. She planted herself firmly between the driver and me. 'You okay, Rosie?' she said from the corner of her mouth.

I nodded. She smelt like strawberries.

'You'll have to move!' shouted the driver. 'I ain't got time for games. I got wages to earn.' He flicked a broad hand at me as if I were a wasp buzzing around his head.

Gran squinted at the driver. Her lips thinned. 'Bobby Dwyer?' she said. 'Ginnie's youngest? I always wondered what became of you.'

Bobby let his hands fall from his hips. He pulled off his helmet and glanced nervously at the bull-dozer and then back at Gran. 'With all due respect, Mrs Nunn, we gotta job to do here. Can't you—?'

'How's your mum doing, Bobby? She's up at the retirement village now, isn't she?' asked Gran.

Bobby shuffled in his big worn boots. He fiddled with his ear and kept his eyes down. He cradled his helmet in one arm like it was a round yellow baby. 'Mrs Nunn, we've got orders. We have to—'

'Be sure to say hello from me next time you visit her, won't you, Bobby?' said Gran, her voice all deep and growly.

Bobby swallowed. 'Yep, yep, sure will.' His voice sounded kind of squeaky. He mumbled something I couldn't hear and then, with a scratch of his head, suggested he get Mr Young from the developer's office. 'You know. Just to sort everythin' out.' He turned to leave. 'Good luck to ya, Mrs Nunn.'

'Yes, thank you, Bobby,' said Gran. 'See you.' We watched him lumber back to his bulldozer and grab his keys before stomping off towards the road. I wished he'd taken the bulldozer. It towered like a huge metal predator over the broken trees.

'Rosie love,' whispered Gran when he'd gone. 'You can't stay here. You heard what Bobby said. They've been told to clear all the trees. It's too late, Rosie. It's going to happen.' She wrapped an arm around my shoulders and squeezed. A fat hot tear rolled down my cheek.

'But Gran, Smooch is back. They'll kill him if they knock down his trees,' I sobbed. 'If I go, they'll bulldoze him.'

Gran shook her head. 'I'm sorry, Rosie. You'll get hurt if you stay here. I know it's awful, but you're going to have to move.'

I opened my mouth to say no but I closed it again when I heard a horrible ear-splitting squeal. Someone was using a chainsaw!

'They're coming from the other side of the creek!' I shouted. 'Stay here. Guard Smooch!' I broke away from Gran and ran towards the sound. I weaved between the trees and shimmied across the log over the creek. Then I saw something that made my breath catch sharply in my throat.

A man with a helmet and a chainsaw stood at the base of a large gum tree. Beside him were two other men and a mulcher. They must have gotten through the fence between the new townhouses and our farm.

'Stop!' I screamed. 'Stop! There's a koala. These are *his* trees!'

It was useless shouting. The men were wearing earmuffs. I waved my arms around wildly, but I was too scared to get any closer. What if the tree they were sawing fell on top of me?

This wasn't supposed to happen. This was exactly what my petition was supposed to stop. Didn't Mrs Glover say they'd have to listen? I stood for a moment, clenching my fists, not sure what to do. Then I turned and sped back to Smooch's tree. Gran was still standing in front of it but she was talking to a man in a black suit. He had a briefcase in one hand and in the other, a smart black clipboard with the words 'Hall and Young Development' plastered across the back.

'Yes, Mr Young, I understand there wasn't a koala here when the council checked,' Gran was saying when I joined her. 'But now there is.' She had to raise her voice to be heard over the chain-saws. She pointed up at Smooch nestled in his tallowwood tree. His big brown eyes were wide open and his mouth was slightly apart. He was panting in fear.

'See? You can't knock it down while he's up there. You'll have to call a stop to the works while we sort this out.'

The chainsaws were getting closer. I felt sick.

Mr Young put down his briefcase. 'All these trees will go eventually,' he said, waving his arm towards the creek. 'What difference does it make? See this one?' He tapped his pen against the trunk of Smooch's tree. 'It's in the middle of a proposed driveway.' He opened his folder and showed Gran some complicated drawings. I leant over to take a look. There were black lines covered with numbers and letters – none of it made any sense.

Gran shook her head and tutted. 'But the driveway could easily have a few bends in it, Mr Young. Surely you can be flexible when . . .'

Then Gran did something incredible. More incredible than scaring off wild dogs. More incredible than standing up to angry bulldozer drivers. She used the words I'd told her from the websites. Words I'd thought she hadn't heard. Words like 'endangered', 'corridors' and 'short-sighted'. Mr

Young answered with different words. He said things like 'budget', 'timeframe' and 'difficult'. All the while, the chainsaws shrieked. They were getting closer and closer. Soon, they'd be right here, right at Smooch's tree.

I sucked in a deep breath and grabbed on to the lower limbs of the tallowwood. I hauled myself up onto the first branch. And then onto the second. I edged upwards and upwards until I found a safe V between the trunk and a branch, just like Smooch. I could see him from where I sat, but couldn't quite reach him. 'Smooch,' I called. 'Smooch, it's okay! I'm here now. I won't let them hurt you.'

But Smooch wasn't listening. He was throwing his head in the air and squealing. And rocking forwards and backwards on his branch.

'Smooch, don't! It'll be alright. I'm going to stop them. I promise.'

I filled my lungs and yelled in the direction of the chainsaws. 'Stop! Stop cutting down the trees!'

Nothing happened.

I tried again. 'Stop!'

Below me Gran and Mr Young kept talking. Over to my right, the chainsaws kept roaring. In the branch above me, Smooch squealed louder.

I cupped my hands around my mouth and screamed with all my might. 'STOP! RIGHT NOW!'

Still nothing. My right foot was getting a cramp. Ants were running up and down the trunk. My voice hurt from shouting. The chainsaws were getting closer . . .

One more time.

'I said STOP!'

Gran swung around. Mr Young leapt sideways. Their heads jerked upwards towards me. Gran's arms flew in the air. They both raced to the foot of the tree. Their mouths moved. Mr Young punched numbers into his phone.

The chainsaws stopped.

12. The City

'Rosie! Come on, love. They've gone now. It's time to get down.' Gran stood beside the tree trunk, not daring to take her eyes off me. Mr Young had gone. The chainsaws had gone. Only Gran was left. She begged and pleaded and even tried shouting a few times. But I still wouldn't come down.

And then Uncle Malcolm arrived. He paced up and down beside Gran, muttering loudly and shaking his head. Glimpses of his green and yellow shorts flashed as he walked. Gran must have called him in the middle of his golf game. Such bright stripy shorts would normally have looked funny, but nothing was very funny today.

'Rosie, I promise you. Uncle Malcolm will make the developers stop. We'll get this whole koala thing sorted out. There's no need for you to guard that tree anymore. Now come on, love. Down you get.'

I didn't move. Adults always say stuff they don't mean when they want you to do something. How did I know the men with the chainsaws had stopped for good? They were probably just having smoko. Any minute now the roaring could start again.

'Rosie, now that's enough, love,' pleaded Gran. 'Come down and I'll make us some sandwiches. There's a girl.'

I still didn't move. Uncle Malcolm was probably over-the-top mad because I'd held up the developers. Mad because I'd made the bulldozers stop when it was him who'd sold the land to them in the first place. Who knew what he'd do if I got down from Smooch's tree.

'Rose, do what your grandmother says! Get down from that tree! This minute!'

So I was right. Uncle Malcolm *was* mad. I was definitely not getting down now.

Smooch was still rocking back and forth on his branch and looked ready to move away. What if he decided to find another tree to hide in? I couldn't spend the rest of my life following him around, protecting every tree he climbed. But I couldn't leave him here either. What should I do? I looked down at Gran. She was still waiting below me, her face growing more anxious by the minute. Uncle Malcolm was crouched beside her, making call after call on his phone. The ground suddenly seemed a long way down. I suddenly seemed a long way up. Why was Gran's face going wavy and in and out of focus? I clasped my branch more firmly and made myself count to 100.

'Ro-ose? Ro-ose? Are you there?' The bushes along the creek began swaying and snapping, like someone was trying to get through. They needn't have bothered. The bulldozer had left a thick ugly scar from the road – they could have easily followed that. Whoever it was, I could hear them talking and calling and arguing all the way, and I craned my neck to have a look. They didn't sound like chainsawers at least. Eventually, five brightly dressed ladies untangled themselves from the vines and creepers and headed towards Smooch's tree.

'Rose! Can you hear me?' Carol sounded out of breath. She and four other women crowded around the base of the tree and stared worriedly up at me. 'We've done up a roster. Me and the other carers. We'll watch over the creek. At least until we can get some guarantees from the developers about the trees. You can come down and go with your gran. Leave it to us, okay?'

'But what if they come back?' I called out, trying not to sound hysterical. 'They could clear the lot by tomorrow.'

'Don't worry,' Carol insisted. 'Take a look at us. No-one will sneak past us in a hurry. We promise we'll keep Smooch safe. Now come on, I think your uncle wants to talk to you.'

I looked at Smooch and then at Carol. She'd been right about everything else so far, and she loved Smooch just as much as I did. Well, nearly as much as me. I knew for sure she wouldn't let anyone hurt him.

'Be brave,' I whispered to Smooch before slithering down the tree. I stood with my head bowed in front of Uncle Malcolm and Gran, waiting for the worst. But there was no worst. Instead Gran took my hand and said gently, 'It's nice to have you back, Rosie.'

At the house I changed out of my pyjamas and met Gran in the kitchen for lunch. 'What does Uncle Malcolm want to talk to me about?' I asked once we'd sat down to eat some sandwiches. Uncle Malcolm was out on the verandah, pacing up and down with his phone pressed to his ear. But Gran wouldn't tell me a thing. It was hopeless trying to interpret her eyeball swivels and wiggly eyebrows. I would just have to wait.

I could hardly sit still until Uncle Malcolm finally came inside. 'Rose, I need you to come with me,' he said, leaning over to give Gran a goodbye kiss. 'I'm taking you to the city. I need to show you something.'

I looked desperately at Gran. She couldn't be serious? Who knew what Uncle Malcolm would do to keep me away from the bulldozers?

I dug my elbows into the table. There was no way I would go. But Gran's face went all crumply. 'Go on,' she said. 'He just wants to help, you'll see.'

I had to go. For Gran.

'You'll be alright, love,' she added as I slid into the passenger seat of Uncle Malcolm's fancy sports car.

As soon as I was buckled up, Uncle Malcolm drove off. He kept his eyes on the road and drove and drove. I tried not to sniffle. I swiped my nose every now and then as I watched the enormous skyscrapers grow closer and closer. I'd only been to the city twice and both times had been scary. But driving there with Uncle Malcolm today was the scariest of all. So much glass and steel and so many peaks of all different shapes and sizes. My head swirled seeing all those buildings towering so high.

Eventually, we exited the freeway and wound around the skinny side streets between the buildings. We only stopped when we came to a massive house with three roller doors and a wide paved driveway.

'Here we are,' Uncle Malcolm said, turning off the engine.

It looked pretty nice for a house so close to the sky-scrapers. Two enormous black dogs sprung towards us when we got out. Black curly hair flopped over their faces, hiding their eyes but not their long pink lolling tongues. Their tails turned into helicopter blades when they saw Uncle Malcolm – wagging around and around in circles as they bounded excitedly about. Uncle Malcolm rubbed his hand absently over the back of the dog with the pink collar. The one with the blue collar sat on my foot. I gave his head a pat. How come Uncle Malcolm had dogs? Wasn't he allergic to . . .

'That's George and this here is Mildred. They're totally harmless, just a little bouncy. Now, come inside, I want to show you something.'

Uncle Malcolm walked on ahead and I dragged my feet after him. I hardly dared to think what he wanted to show me. He stopped at the front door to take off his yellow and red lace-up golf shoes. Once I'd taken off my shoes, he opened the door and motioned me inside. I followed him in silence, wishing Lizzie were with me to make me brave. The whole house was white. All the walls were white. All the floors were white. All the chairs were white. Everything was white except the plump red cushions propped neatly on the couches.

Finally, Uncle Malcolm led me into the kitchen. He pushed a grey cat off one of the kitchen stools and pointed for me to sit down. Another cat eyed me suspiciously from the windowsill. Both of them had enormous pointy ears – ears almost twice the size you'd expect a cat to have. I could hardly believe it. First dogs, now cats? I wondered what other animals Uncle Malcolm might have stashed in the backyard.

Like the rest of the house, the kitchen was spotless. The benchtop was almost as big as Gran's double bed and was so clean it glimmered like a sheet of polished ice. There was nothing on it except for a shiny metal bowl filled with plastic oranges. I wondered why they were plastic ones, not real ones. Perhaps Uncle Malcolm was allergic to fruit too.

He pulled up a stool and sat down beside me. 'So, you see now, there's no need to go hiding up trees. You and Gran will be perfectly comfortable here. There's plenty of room for the two of you, and I'm positive you'll like it more than you think. I've got wireless internet and Foxtel and I . . .'

So this was his way of tricking me? Making me think he was nice, that his house was nice, so I'd agree to move to the city with him? Well, he was wrong. I knew better than to fall for that. I was considering demanding he drive me home when the grey cat sprung onto my lap and let me stroke his warm head. He was the same colour as Smooch and just as soft. What was happening to Smooch while I sat here? What if he was already dead? My throat tightened. Before I could stop it, a huge sob escaped my lips.

'What is it? Tell me what's wrong.'

I didn't want to tell Uncle Malcolm. Someone like him would never understand. But then the cat on my lap tipped its head up and licked away my leaking tears with its small scratchy tongue. The way Lizzie used to lick them. My lips trembled. Lizzie was gone. Mum was gone. And Dad was gone too.

What if Smooch was next?

I ended up telling Uncle Malcolm the whole story. Surprisingly, he listened quietly without interrupting, although he got up a couple of times to pass me tissues.

'I see,' he said when I'd finished. He poured us both a drink of water and handed me a sparkling crystal glass. 'You're right. All that tree clearing has become quite a problem in places like Cleveland and Wellington Point. They're so beautiful that everyone wants to live there, but after all those new houses are built, they're not beautiful anymore.'

I nodded and blew my nose.

'Okay, well, here's what we're going to do,' Uncle Malcolm said briskly. 'Mr Bantex, the mayor of the Bay district, and I were playing golf this morning when your gran called me. We were about to tee off from the eighth hole . . .' He cleared his throat and scratched the top of his forehead. He frowned. 'You made your gran very worried, you know.'

I squirmed in my seat. I hadn't meant to worry Gran. She had enough problems to deal with.

'Anyway, after what you've just told me, I think it might be worth giving him a call. Perhaps I could arrange for the two of you to meet?'

I put down the plastic orange I'd been fiddling with. I didn't know what was more astonishing: Uncle Malcolm knowing the Mayor of Redland Bay, or me possibly meeting him.

'It sounds like you've got a whole swag of ideas about how we could save your koala,' Uncle Malcolm said. 'Why don't we see if Mayor Bantex can help you with them? He's a good man, I'm sure he would listen. What do you think? Rose?'

I opened my mouth but no words came out.

'Perhaps you could even give a short presentation about your proposals. We could ask a representative from Hall and Young Development to come along and one or two of the councillors. Perhaps even your local State Member. What do you think?'

A presentation! Proposals! I couldn't possibly give a presentation. 'But I'm useless at public speaking,' I squeaked. 'What will I say?'

'Well, for one, you can't just front up and tell the mayor, the councillors and the developers that they can't have progress. You'll need to show them how it can be done to suit everyone: you, the developers and your koala. You need to offer alternatives. We should arrange this as soon as possible. Before any more damage can be done. What about Friday? That gives you two days to prepare.'

'Friday?' I nearly shouted. My head went all woozy. I couldn't speak to the mayor on Friday! I needed more time. 'But I thought you hated animals.'

Uncle Malcolm looked shocked. 'Whatever gave you that idea? Of course I don't hate animals. I'm allergic to most of them, that's all. George and Mildred are giant poodles – strictly hypo-allergenic. And the cats are hairless sphynxs. So you see, animals suit me just fine. I mean, I'm not offering to cuddle your smelly little koala or anything and you're certainly not bringing him here. I just don't want you hiding in trees and worrying your grand-mother half to death. After all the stress the sale has caused her, the least I can do is help. Besides, your dad loved that creek. So . . . what do you think?'

I hardly had time to worry about Smooch for the rest of the week. Uncle Malcolm and I were too busy preparing my speech. He came over in the afternoon and helped me make a ton of phone calls. We spoke to everyone we could think of who might give us some ideas for Smooch's creek. We googled 'safe koala development' on Uncle Malcolm's laptop and found a place in New South Wales where they'd built a new housing estate without destroying koala trees. They sent us copies of their newsletters and spoke to us about the things that worked in their development, and the things that didn't. There were more ideas on the koala websites I'd found and Uncle Malcolm even lent me his expensive camera to take photos of Smooch to add to the presentation.

By Friday, my speech was ready. All I had to do was make sure I didn't muck it up.

13. The Mayor

Gran ironed a crisp clean shirt for me to wear on Friday. When I was dressed, she clipped a little furry koala to my collar. 'From Smooch and me,' she said, smiling. 'For good luck.' Then she cooked an extra-big portion of scrambled eggs to get me off to a good start. My stomach was jumping around so much I could hardly face eating them. But I ate them anyway, just to see the satisfied look on Gran's face.

And then it was time.

Uncle Malcolm pulled up just after eight. He'd

taken the day off work especially. And he'd dressed in a smart grey suit with a bright red tie.

Gran sat with me in the back of Uncle Malcolm's car and held my hand while I practised my presentation over and over in my head. It didn't take long to get to the council chambers. I wished Uncle Malcolm would make another trip around the block. Only I still wouldn't have been ready. I'd never be ready.

I thought I might be sick as we climbed the steps to the front entrance. I gripped Gran's hand so hard I probably cut off the blood flow.

People were standing all around, waving banners that said things like, *Stop the Destruction* and *Save Our Koalas*. Some of the people were even chanting, like the protests I'd seen on TV. A group of school kids held a sign that said, *No Trees, No Me*. The writing was so neat it looked like one of the fonts in Microsoft Word.

'Mrs Glover?' I whispered. The sign lowered. Mrs Glover's beaming face appeared behind it. Shuffling around her to get a better look were the grinning faces of my whole entire class. Even Tahlia and Kellee were there. 'Good luck!' they chorused as we passed.

I spotted Carol by the doors, talking to a couple of reporters. I hoped her friends were still guarding Smooch's trees. She turned to give me a wink and I was sure they were keeping Smooch safe.

And then we went in. Everyone smiled at me and I concentrated on smiling back without throwing up. The swirly pattern on the carpet didn't help. I managed to get to where Mayor Bantex was standing without my legs collapsing, but my throat was dry and my hand was cold and clammy when he shook it.

'Welcome Rose,' he said in a friendly voice. 'I've been looking forward to meeting you.'

'Thank you,' I peeped. I pulled my USB out of my pocket and gave it to him with a trembling hand. He passed it over to his assistant and introduced me to the other councillors and to Bill Young from Hall and Young Development. I told him we'd already met – kind of. Then Mayor Bantex said, 'Over to you, Rose.'

I took a deep breath. I glanced at Gran. She smiled and nodded. I looked at Uncle Malcolm and then over to Carol by the door. She gave me the thumbs up and I began.

'Good morning Mayor Bantex, Mr Young, councillors, ladies and gentlemen, and distinguished guests. Thank you for having me here this morning.'

It came out exactly like I'd practised. No squeaks, no mistakes. I was doing it! I was speaking in public. I clicked on the first slide. It was a photograph of Smooch and I explained how we'd rescued him. My stomach stopped churning and I clicked on the next slide. It showed a picture of a cleared block of land – not a tree in sight. No-one laughed. No-one told me to stop. Mayor Bantex and Mr Young and every councillor sat glued to my PowerPoint presentation.

At the end, they all clapped. Even Mayor Bantex! Especially Mayor Bantex. Then they asked me lots of questions and when I'd finished answering those, everyone went out onto the verandah for cake, lemonade and cups of tea. I couldn't stop smiling.

When it was time to leave, Mayor Bantex's assistant escorted us outside and the crowd around the entrance cheered. Mrs Glover stepped forward as I passed the *No Tree, No Me* banner. 'Congratulations, Rose,' she said before pausing and tapping a finger thoughtfully to her chin. 'I think you've well and truly earned yourself an 'A', don't you? Well done, young lady!'

'What now?' said Gran, when we were back home and sitting around the kitchen table.

'Now we have to wait,' I explained. 'The councillors and developers have to discuss my ideas and see what they can do. Mayor Bantex said there is no guarantee anything will change.'

'I'm so proud of you, Rosie,' said Gran. 'You're a chip off the old block. Your dad would have been proud of you too.'

'Yes, he would've been thrilled to see you fighting for his beloved creek,' said Uncle Malcolm. 'Quite the animal-lover your dad. Looks like you've got the animal gene too.'

14. Change

Waiting to hear back about the development took forever. I practically wore out the path to our letterbox I checked it that much. Gran said a watched mailbox was like a watched kettle. She gave me extra chores to keep me away from it, but that didn't really help.

Finally, the letter we'd been waiting for arrived. Gran called Uncle Malcolm and he came over as soon as he could. Gran bustled around making tea while I offered Uncle Malcolm some scones.

Then Gran gave the big white envelope to me. I ripped it open and peered nervously inside.

'Come on, Rosie. What does it say?'

With shaking hands, I pulled out a crisp A4 letter and a booklet titled, *Proposed Changes to the Development of Lot 3425, Wellington Point.*

I read the letter out loud.

Dear Rose,

Thank you so much for showing us that koalas are not the only ones who love beautiful trees. Here at Hall and Young Development, we can all remember climbing a few in our day. You have reminded us how precious places like Wellington Point are and have shown us that we need to protect the things we love.

We hope you will approve of the proposals outlined in the enclosed document, and if you have any questions or suggestions, please feel free to call me anytime on my direct line.

Yours sincerely,

Mr William Young

I frowned. 'That's good, isn't it?'

'Yes,' laughed Uncle Malcolm. 'It's great.' He picked up the booklet and flicked it open. 'See. Here are all the things they're suggesting. Just like you asked.' He pointed to the long list of dot points as Gran and I huddled excitedly around him.

'Fewer houses. Wide gaps left for koala trees. Koala-friendly fences with poles to help koalas and other wildlife get around. Look, there's even a clause that says hollow logs must be left in place for creatures to hide in. This is perfect, Rose, exactly what you wanted!'

The proposals also said that koalas at risk were not to be relocated, but were to be encouraged to stay by planting appropriate trees. Smooch's favourite tree would stay, with the new driveway being built well away from it, not through it, as originally planned.

Gran looked at me with a satisfied smile. 'Congratulations, Rosie, you did it!' she said. 'Now everyone wins. The developers, the koalas, and people who love animals like you and me. Well done!'

We had some more tea and another round of scones. That's when Uncle Malcolm told us he had some more good news. Brilliant news, in fact. Gran and I leant forward in our seats.

'Do you remember the developers had a hiccup? A problem delaying development around the house?'

Gran and I nodded.

'Well, they were having trouble getting approval to remove the house. Mayor Bantex decided to take it a step further. It turns out this house is so old it's of historic importance to the area. He suggested I apply for it to be "heritage-listed".'

Gran nearly spilled her tea. '"Heritage-listed"?'

'It means this house was one of the first built in the area. Something like 1870, I think. The first farmers in the region lived around here. A house as old as this is so historically important that it can't be knocked down. So it looks like you can stay!'

'Wahoo!' I yelled. I bounced up and hugged Uncle Malcolm around the neck. He started a little but I was too busy saying thank you over and over again to care. When I finally let go, Uncle Malcolm coughed awkwardly and straightened his tie.

'But how will that work?' said Gran, still looking unsure. 'Will I have to rent the house from these history people?'

'No, no, not at all. We're adjusting the paperwork so that the developers will still build on the farm, but you will own the house. You won't be able to knock down any walls or change the outside of the house too much, but you will be able to keep the small yards for the animals and—'

'So Mickey and Sally and the chooks can stay?' I chirped happily.

'Yes, yes, the animals can stay.' He paused and looked over at Gran. 'So, what do you say?'

There was only one thing to say. Yes, yes, YES! I ran down to tell Smooch as soon as Uncle Malcolm had gone.

'Smooch!' I cried, gazing up into his tallowwood tree. 'We did it! We really did it!'

Smooch was curled up fast asleep and didn't move.

'Now, you'll have to get used to sharing this place. It'll still be your backyard and everything, but it won't be quite the same. There'll be more houses, and more dogs, and loads more cars. You're going to have to be careful.'

I sighed and leant my back against the rough bark of the tree. Who would believe it? Little old me, standing up to all those people.

I closed my eyes.

It was true what Gran always said. You don't have to be big to be special. The breeze in the treetops agreed.

What should you do if you find an injured koala?

When Rose and Gran found Smooch's mother, and then Smooch, it was quite a scary situation. Not only were they confronted with a pack of blood-hungry dogs, but there was also an injured koala's life hanging in the balance. If you ever find an injured koala, it's important that you know what to do. Here are some steps that you can follow:

- First, check for danger. Will you be safe if you help out? If you're alone or with friends, call an adult or a teacher to assist you.

- Keep other animals away and don't try to pick up or touch the koala (unless advised otherwise by the koala rescuers). It's also really important to keep calm and quiet because koalas stress very easily.

- Next, make sure the koala needs rescuing (maybe it's actually okay). You could do this by watching the koala for a minute to see if it's just resting or trying to find its way.

- If the koala is in trouble and on the ground, place a washing basket or something similar on top of it to keep it safe. Stay nearby until rescuers come.

- Don't try to feed the koala, but providing a bowl of water may be a good idea – ask the rescuers for advice.
- Even if the koala's not moving, there may be a joey inside, so please ask an adult to call for help. You could try the RSPCA on 1300 ANIMAL or call your vet for the number of your nearest wildlife organisation, such as the National Parks and Wildlife Service. Or you could try a postcode search on www.fauna.org.au to find a nearby wildlife carer.
- Lastly, you could store the right rescue number for your area in your phone just in case!

How you can help koalas

Like Rose, everyone can help save our koalas! If you live in a koala area you could:
- Keep native gum trees in your yard.
- Ask your parents and friends to drive carefully and watch for wildlife on the roads, especially at night or in low light.
- Keep your dogs and cats inside at night. Even small dogs can hurt koalas and other native animals.

- Ask your parents to build koala-friendly fences.

Or, like Rose, if you discover an issue you could:
- Write letters to politicians and newspapers urging them to make koala conservation a priority. You could even draw up a petition.
- Report koala sightings in your local area.
- Organise a fun run to raise money for research and rehabilitation.
- Start a tree planting program at your school.
- Check out the websites below for more information and ideas.

Useful websites

www.savethekoala.com

The Australian Koala Foundation is the main non-profit organisation in Australia dedicated to the conservation and management of wild koalas and their habitats. This website has information on what you can do to help save koalas, including fundraising ideas, koala spotting and tree planting information.

www.wildlifewarriors.org.au

Australia Zoo Wildlife Warriors support injured, threatened or endangered wildlife in Australia and worldwide. Their website gives an insight into their wildlife hospital, how they fundraise and how everyday people (like you!) can make a difference.

www.kids.nationalgeographic.com

National Geographic Kids has great stories and pictures about animals from all over the world and details how people are trying to help them. There are also lots of activities, games and interesting facts.

www.wwf.org.au

WWF-Australia promotes conservation and protection of critical areas and species around the world. Their site is jammed full of information on all sorts of animals, their environments, and ways we can help preserve our beautiful planet.

www.ehp.qld.gov.au/wildlife/daisyhill-centre/

The Daisy Hill Koala Centre is a free information centre located near Brisbane. Their website has heaps of information about koalas including what to do if you find a sick or injured koala and how to make your yard koala-friendly, plus some great activity sheets. They also offer education programs for schools about koala conservation.

Fun koala facts

Did you know that . . .

- A baby koala is the size of a jellybean when it is born and is called a joey?
- Koalas sleep for around 20 hours and eat about two shopping bags of leaves a day?
- Koalas have spotty backsides so that they can't be seen from the ground?
- Koalas have unique fingerprints . . . just like humans!

Acknowledgements

A heartfelt thank you to my friends and family for all of the conversations starting with, 'Now, about my book . . .' In particular, thank you to my wonderful husband Don, beautiful daughters Bethany and Charlotte, my parents Joan and Chris, and the wild card, a secret literary fan, my brother Ralph.

Thank you to my patient and invaluable critiquing friends, Marci Dahlenburg and Ann Harth, who read and re-read my stories with remarkable enthusiasm and tact. I am also grateful to Debbie Pointing from the Koala Action Group, Jeff Regan from Paradise Country, Wayne from Wellington Point Farm, Natalie from Ascot Demolition and Glenda Emmerson for their help with technical matters; to Deborah Tabart OAM, Chief Executive Officer, Australian Koala Foundation for her support and enthusiasm; and to Kristen Collie from the Daisy Hill Koala Park, Jill Richardson from the Australian Koala Foundation and Bridget Chenoweth from

Australia Zoo Wildlife Warriors, for their generous contributions to the factual pages of this book.

A big warm hug to my students in the Ronald McDonald Learning Program, whose perseverance and courage inspired Rose in the first place.

And finally, to the amazing team at UQP. What a fabulous experience to be published by you. Thanks to Kristy Bushnell (project editor), Aileen Lord (cover design and artwork) and to the talented Cathy Vallance (editor), for finding all the 'gasps' and 'hugs' (and much more) in the manuscript. And thanks to Kristina Schulz (publisher) for believing in me.